Blood Renegades

BR, Volume 1

Ashley Casey Tyrrell

Published by Ashley Casey Tyrrell, 2023.

BLOOD RENEGADES

First edition. May 30, 2023.

ISBN: 979-8223854722

Written by Ashley Casey Tyrrell.

Table of Contents

PROLOGUE

"BRING HER HERE!!!" A loud, booming voice could be heard throughout the castle. The person who shouted that is a tall man wearing a dark suit with a blue tie, he also has very dark blue hair which is covering part of his eyes.

"Yes Your Majesty" Two armed people wearing a mask which looks like a giant, open mouth ready to swallow and eat anything it sees fit, the people are also wearing a dark blazer, similar to the one that the king was wearing, however, their ties and shirts are a different colour to the king's with their ties all being red and their shirts all being white, each guard also has very spiky dark brown hair and they all stand up straight.

Upon hearing the king's orders, two of the guards in the area rush out of the room looking to grab someone.

Soon, the guards come back in with a scruffily dressed woman scared look in her face, the king bends down and starts talking to her. "Now, now Megan, I have my sources that you've been helping the rebellion to try and take me down, I'm hurt, I considered you a friend Megan." From the 'I'm hurt' the King speaks in a sarcastic tone, indicating that he did not consider Megan a friend.

"Y..y..y...you did?" Megan asks with a shaking breath and sounding like she's about to cry.

The king bursts into laughter and ends up rolling on the ground, it takes him around 30 seconds to regain his composure before he talks again. "NO!!! Why would you even think that I'd be friends with a common peasant like you?" The king's tone changes from one of laughter to one of seriousness then starts to walk to his throne, clearly looking for something.

"But...but...but...I'm friends with your sist-" Megan cuts herself off before she can finish that sentence and upon hearing that, the king stops moving, turns around and goes back to Megan.

"What....Did....You....Just.....Say?" The tone of the king is indicating that he is now starting to get pissed off and annoyed with Megan.

"...." Megan stays silent, she knows that whatever she says next won't be good in the slightest.

"I'll give you a few more chances to answer me." The king says that in a calm tone, after which Megan spits in his face.

"Rot in hell, I'd much rather die than tell you what I know." Megan says that in a still scared but this time also determined tone and the king goes back to his throne, goes behind it and gets a sword out.

"It's a shame it had to be like this Megan, if you had just simply told me what you know, I would have let you live" The king says that in a calm tone as well. "GUARDS, Get the camera crew here NOW!!!" The King says that in an ordering tone.

"Yes Your Majesty, right away sir!!!" Multiple guards run off somewhere.

"While we wait for them, let's continue our little chat shall we?" The King's tone suddenly changes from the ordering one from a few seconds back to a more calm and composed one.

"You know, my offer is still out there Megan, if you tell me what you know then I will let you live."

"AS IF!!!" Megan says that in a scared tone as well.

"It's a shame you know, in a different timeline, we may have been friends Megan, I doubt it but with an infinite number of universes, you never know, hell, there may even be one where you're running this country." The king is speaking in a calm tone now, it's clear that he is just doing this to buy some time.

"W...w...what do you mean?" Megan is now speaking in a soft tone, it's clear that she knows what's going to happen in a few minutes and instead of fighting, has just come to terms with it.

"Do you know of the multiverse theory Megan?" The king asks.

"N..n...no." She replies in the same soft tone as before.

"The short version of it is that there are an infinite number of universes that exist right outside ours and each one is very different, sometimes they're only slightly different, other times the differences are massive, you still with me?" The king says that in a calm tone, due to the tone of his voice, it's clear that he seems to try and have a casual chat with everyone he's about to execute.

"Y..y...yeah, I am." She replies.

"Good, continuing on from that, sometimes those differences can range from our roles being swapped to roles being the same but replaced with other things instead of us humans and everything in between, literally anything you can think of, in a multiverse, there is likely a different version of it somewhere." As soon as the king finishes saying that, the guards that left the room come back with a camera crew, the camera crew look the same as the guards.

"Ah, you're here, well Megan, that was a nice chat, but I'm afraid it's time for you to say goodbye."

The king says readying his sword.

"We're recording now Your Majesty." One of the camera crew says.

"Greetings my loyal citizens, I trust you've all been well?" He says to the camera.

A very dim but still audible booing sound can be heard from the throne room.

"I take that as a yes, anyway I have a special treat for you all today." The king moves away from the camera and goes to the other side of Megan.

"Now, you all know I usually use my gun for these executions but, today I decided I should use my sword for a special reason, well actually...Megan, I will give you one more chance to live, use it and i'll cut off the broadcast and let you leave alive....what do you know about my sister?" The king is still speaking in a calm tone.

Instead of saying anything, Megan spits on him then replies "Rot in hell dickface".

"Aww Megan, I was hoping you'd give up what you know, oh well, any last words for anyone out there before I do this?" The king asks

"...No." She replies.

"Oh? That's strange, usually, everyone does have last words, anyway, I'm not complaining" He says.

In one swift swing, the king decapitates Megan sending her head flying across the room, not only that but also the body going limp and sending blood all over the floor from her neck, not only that but the head flying is also leaving blood on both the floor and walls of the throne room.

"Dispose of the body." He says in a sinister tone while holding the bloody sword, with bits of the blood dripping onto the floor.

"See that, this is one of two possible deaths for anyone who dares to disobey my rules and one more thing...If anyone manages to capture the rebellion and bring them to me ALIVE then I will grant that person and a friend of theirs full immunity and make them next in line for the throne."

The broadcast cuts off and the king is still in the throne room.

"Dispose of the body and clean this" He gives the sword to one of the guards and they rush off to clean it, two more grab a hold of the body and walk it away, meanwhile the king sits down on his throne, looking outside of his window.

"Where the fuck are you hiding Kingston, I know you're down there somewhere, I just need you dead then I can go through with my master plan." He says speaking to himself.

Chapter 1: Hope Part 1

Everyone saw what just happened with Megan, the king decapitated her live on TV for thousands of people to watch live and all throughout the kingdom, there was fear and shock in the eyes of every citizen....except for a few special ones, hidden in the capital in a seemingly average and innocent enough looking house is a rebellion, a rebellion with the intentions on overthrowing the king and their leader: Hope Kingston, a tough no nonsense yet relaxed at the same time young woman, although except for one person, no one knows Hope's personal reasons for wanting to dethrone the king, only her public ones which are the same as every other rebel member.

"Ms Ki- I mean Hope, we've just received an update." A pink-haired person says, they are wearing a leather biker outfit, complete with gloves, however on their face, they have a headset, presumably to communicate with Hope and the rebels whenever she goes out.

"Oh? Do tell Megan." The young woman looks over to the pink-haired person, although her eyesight is obstructed by her hockey mask, there is an earpiece that is dangling from her left ear, presumably, it's so that she can communicate with rebels, alongside that, she has messy blue hair which was styled so that it doesn't completely get in the way of her eyes, attached to the back of her jean jacket was an assault rifle which is most likely used when combating the king's guards, however under her jean jacket is a white plain hoodie with nothing too outstanding about it, on her legs, she has slightly ripped but still easily usable jeans on along with army style combat boots.

"Because of the decapitation a few minutes ago, the king's guards are currently preoccupied, we may have the chance to at least scout the castle looking for possible entrances!" Megan says, sounding determined.

"That may be true, however, we don't know how many are currently preoccupied and whether or not that changes the number of guards on sight anytime someone is executed, plus we also don't know if guard rotations change per execution, knowing him...I wouldn't be surprised if the rotation does change." She replies, clear disappointment in her voice, it's clear to both her and Megan that she wanted to scout the castle but it may very well be for nothing because no one can tell when the next execution will be.

"I get that you wanted to do this Megan, I really do, hell I want to do it as well but logic says otherwise." She says with the same disappointed tone in her voice.

Megan sighs "I understand Hope" There's a look of sadness in her eyes, but it doesn't seem to be from the rejection of the scouting and Hope notices this.

"Hey, you ok Megan?" She asks in a calm and comforting voice.

Hearing that caught Megan off guard, she knows that Hope considers her a friend but still is not used to it. "Y...y...yeah, I am, it's just that..." She trails off, indicating that a part of her does want to talk about whatever's on her mind but another part doesn't.

"Hey Megan, it's ok." Hope pulls Megan into a hug "You don't have to talk about it if you don't want to, just take your time and tell me when you're ready because I know how hard it is to say things you want to say but can't bring myself to, hell I spent around 4 months before I was ready to tell you the truth." she says in that same calming and comforting voice as before.

"Y...y...y...you really mean that Hope?" There are tears starting to form in her eyes and stream down Megan's face.

"Yes I do, every single word, just take your time Megan and tell me when you're ready to tell me." Hope replies.

Instead of replying, Megan starts crying in the hug and Hope just continues hugging them to let her cry.

Soon after, Megan stops crying and looks up at hope. "You ok there Megan? That sounded like you really needed to let it out."

Instead of saying anything, she just nods sadly.

"Well, remember what I said and anytime you want to talk about something, i'm here for you, ok?" Hope says in the same calm and comforting voice she's been speaking to Megan in.

Yet again, she just nods instead of saying anything.

"And Megan, I have something to say to you." She

"Huh?" They respond with.

Hope then whispers something into Megan's ear, and when they hear what was whispered, her eyes go from one of sadness to a look of extreme happiness and joy and instead of responding, Megan just tightens her grip on Hope in the hug with Hope returning the hug again.

"Thank you, Hope." Megan says with happiness in her voice.

"You're welcome, Megan." The two then part from the hug and go back to the serious way they were before as they hear a door open.

In the room comes a guy with bright red hair, that's slightly messy, although definitely not as messy as Hope's hair, a white lab coat that goes all the way down to his shoes which are white and blue trainers, however those trainers do look like they have seen better days, under those trainers, he's wearing light blue socks that seem to stretch all the way to the knees, over those though he has smart trousers on which unlike the trainers, look like they've just been worn for the first time and above that, as a dark blue shirt which much like the trousers, looks brand new and amongst all of that, on his face, he's wearing a gas mask which is dark blue, silver, yellow and pink.

"Hope, the new prototype ATV is all ready for you to come and have a look at, same with the new BT-43 sniper rifle/machine gun mix." The guy says.

"Thank you, Henry." Hope replies.

"You're welcome Hope, now if you and Megan just follow me, I can show you both the prototype vehicle and the weapon" He starts walking with the two.

"While the vehicle isn't anywhere near done, the weapon is nearly done, however before we can produce it and give it to all of you, there do need to be a bunch of field tests for it so i'm afraid that no matter what you say, I cannot give it to you yet, also you both will be interested to know that we are currently developing a series of bullets that may just be able to break through the castle windows, HOWEVER, there's a but." Henry says that while walking with Hope and Megan down a hallway that looks like it's from a school, there doesn't seem to be much of note there except for a few locked rooms but those are just the rooms which the rebels sleep in at night.

"There's always a but." Hope replies.

"There is a catch, I'm going to need someone to sneak up to a castle window and slightly crack it, allowing yourself to get one bit of glass from it and then sneak back out without getting caught, however, I will only recommend you do that one if you plan to assassinate the king if not then don't bother, the risk will be too high."

"Got it, also we have yet to come up with a plan to overthrow him," Megan responds

"Can't say I blame you, overthrowing a monarch...yeah, at least 100 easier things come to mind straight away," Henry responds

"Yeah but if we're to be successful then it's gonna be all worth it in the end, we can turn what the king made around and maybe even into a utopia." Hope says.

"True, however, looking on the realistic side of things first; we'd need to undo all the damage that The King has done as well as improve relations with other countries because lord above knows that he's....not exactly been the best for multi-country relationships." Henry adds

"Plus, we would also need to get this country opened up to tourism and immigration again because as of right now, there is no way in or out of the country legally." He continues.

"I know that, plus you were the one who made it possible so that people can escape Henry and I feel like they really appreciate it." Hope says.

"Yeah same, I intentionally put that escape where it is because I know that by boat, it'll take around 2 hours to get to the neighbouring country where the citizens who you bring to me to escape can live happy lives and I'm so glad that the immigration department of the country is allowing this, do you think they know what's going on over here?" Henry asks.

"Maybe, Megan, are you able to get us international news sources?" Hope asks.

"I can try and get the BBC, ITV, ABC, and APB news stations, I know it's not many." She replies.

"Hey, I don't mind, do you need any special equipment?" Hope asks.

"Yeah, I'm gonna need a satellite dish, a signal extender and a TV." she says.

"Well, we have a TV in the hideout, I don't know where you're gonna get a satellite dish and a signal extender from though." Hope replies.

"I know where she can get both from but it's not gonna be easy to get them, however, it is a lot less risky than just going to the castle and stealing that one." Henry responds.

"Oh? What is it?" Both Megan and Hope ask.

"Easy, a few houses down, lives one of the castle guards, right now they're most likely working but considering the time." Henry points to a clock on the wall which says "19:45" They're most likely coming home soon because that guard is on the afternoon rotation." Henry responds with.

"Ah, I see, how long do we have?" Megan asks.

"Around 15-20 minutes." Henry replies.

"I'll be out in 14." Megan replies and with that, she's gone.

Henry sighs "Anyway Hope, we're here." Henry unlocks the door to his work room and opens it, inside the room are a bunch of projects currently in creation, each being worked on by multiple workers, however in the centre of the room is a regular-looking ATV, alongside those, there's also multiple monitors, each of which shows a bunch of complex sciency stuff most likely explaining each project's progress and information about them, Hope examines the ATV.

"What's so special about it Henry?" She asks with curiosity in her voice.

"A few things, firstly I'll show off the thing that we know for sure works 100%, if you would just stand in that yellow box." He says.

"Ooooooookkkkkkkkk?" Confused, Hope stands in the box and Henry goes behind a laptop that's on a stand and presses a few buttons, when those buttons have been pressed, the ATV's lights activate and the engine turns on.

Hope is just standing there, now knowing what's gonna happen and knowing that she's gonna be safe, around 30 seconds later, the ATV starts speeding towards her and is able to come to a complete stop right before hitting her, Henry presses a few buttons on the keyboard, it reverses then the engine turns off and the lights deactivate.

"So what do you think?" Henry asks,

"I won't lie right now, I was scared a bit, even though I know, you know what you're doing." Hope responds.

"Yeah, I'd be scared too if I saw that coming towards me, however, I'd be even more scared if I was one of the king's guards." He responds.

"Oh? Why so?" Hope asks.

"Simple, I've not made any code or modifications for it to stop when it detects one of the guards." He answers with a smug smile on his face.

"So, what you're saying is that I can run over the king's guards with this thing." She asks

Instead of responding, he just gives a nod.

"However, there is another thing that's special about it that is still in the developmental phase." He says with a serious tone to his voice.

"And that is?" Hope asks.

"The anti-gravity system." Henry responds.

"Henry, did I just hear you correctly? Did you just say anti-gravity?" Hope asks with a lot of surprise in her voice.

"Yes you did, however, we've really only gotten it to work very few times right now, most of the time it either just crashes into the wall or slightly goes up it but falls back down." Henry responds with a mix of sadness and determination in his voice.

"But, there are a few more special things about it." He says.

"Like what?" She asks.

"Pass me your gun." He says.

She does that.

"Now sit on the ATV and press the red button in the middle of the handlebars." He says

"Alrighty then." She does so and coming up from the wheels of the ATV is a cabin for it once the cabin is completely set up and put in place, Henry starts firing the gun, however ALL of the bullets just bounce off the cabin and after one ammo clip has been used, Henry puts the gun down and Hope disables the cabin by pressing the button.

"Ok...that...is...AMAZING" Hope says as she's standing up to pick up her gun.

"Oh and a great thing about it; is the glass is special and by that I mean you can fire your gun from the inside and it'll hit whatever you're aiming at....well...results may vary depending on what your aim is like when moving at high speeds" Henry responds.

"That is fucking amazing Henry." Hope responds.

"Although, I do have a question." She adds on.

"And that is?" Henry asks.

"Megan has a special disguise that she sometimes uses when going on spy missions, would it know that, that's her or would it just mistake the disguise for a normal guard?" Hope asks.

"Well, on the off chance that situation does arise then yeah, I've programmed it to stop when Megan has her disguise on and it detects it's about to hit her." Henry responds with.

"Ok, that's good." Hope says.

"Now, do you want to see something more complete than that ATV?" Henry asks

"You mean the BT-40?" Hope asks.

"Close, the BT-40 is something secret I'm working on that I'll hopefully be able to show you soon, what I'm referring to is the BT-43 AKA, the sniper rifle/machine gun combo." Henry responds

"Ooooh." Hope responds

Henry takes Hope to the other side of the workroom which has a gun on a table in the middle, at first glance the gun looks like a normal sniper rifle, but upon closer inspection, there's a little switch on the of the gun, just above the trigger, Hope flicks it out of curiosity and the gun instantly changes to a machine gun, however there's a third setting on the switch and yet again, Hope's curiosity got the better of her and flicks it.

When she does flick it, the scope from the sniper comes back out and a second trigger plus an ammo slot appears.

"That's cool." Hope says.

"Heh, thanks Hope, why not take it for a spin using that target over there." Henry points to a typical red and white target that is often found in gun ranges, Hope then picks up the gun and aims it.

"The trigger and ammo clip closest to you is the machine gun part, the one furthest from you is the sniper rifle." Henry says, advising Hope on which is which.

Firstly, she fires the machine gun part at the target and is able to hit it with relative ease, next she tries to aim it with the scope, however, her hands start shaking, it's clear that for some reason, she's nervous.

"Hope, take deep breaths and calm down, I know that you've never used a sniper rifle before but that bit of the gun is always optional, you don't have to use it if you don't want to ." Henry says.

She takes a deep breath then fires the gun via the sniper rifle part, the bullet hits the target dead in the middle, Hope then puts the gun back on the table.

"Damn Hope, you're a natural." Henry says.

"Heh, thanks Henry." She replies.

"So, is there anything else you want to show?" Hope asks

"No but Megan should be ba-" Before henry can finish the sentence, Megan enters the room with the satellite dish and signal extension in hand.

"Told ya, I could do it in 14 minutes." Hope and Henry both look up at the clock: "19:59"

"So Henry, do you mind if I work on this thing in here?" Megan asks.

"Sure, let me just free up some space in an area we haven't used in a while" Henry responds.

"It'll take me around an hour so I'll come up to collect you when ready?" Henry asks.

"Nah, I have nothing to do." Megan says that while shyly looking at Hope, however even though she looks at Hope, neither her nor Henry notice that. "So would it be ok if I helped you?" She asks

"I don't mind the help, we're just gonna need somewhere safe for these until we're done." Henry says.

"Oh, I can look after them for an hour." Hope responds.

"Oh, that would be swell, Hope." After saying that, Megan gives Hope the satellite dish and signal extension and once she has them, she walks out of the workroom and back to her room.

After sitting down, playing games in the base on a game console and keeping an eye on the components, Hope hears a knock on the door, answers it and sees Henry and Megan standing on the other side.

"Right, we're done, wanna come and see it?" Megan asks

"Don't you need to bring it up here in order to use it?" Hope responds

"Not if everything was done correctly, here, take this Hockface." Henry says as he hands a small thing to Hope.

"Hockface?" Hope responds in a confused tone.

"Temporary rebel name, until you can think of a better one yourself." Henry responds.

"I see, well I don't mind the rebels calling me Hope but what about the media...I'll be able to think of that later, what do you want me to do with this?" She asks

"Stick it outside on the wall, preferably on one of the two corners you're facing so as to not arouse suspicion from anyone." Megan responds.

"Got it" With that, Hope walks out of the base, and goes around the side of it but before she goes to the corner, she stops and strokes something that's covered by some light blue tarp, said thing is in the shape of a car.

"Soon, you're almost done." She says in a hushed tone of voice, after stroking it for a bit, she continues walking down the mess of the driveway, in said mess there are tools lying down everywhere, as well as one rebel working on some stuff and another just sitting against the wall.

looking deep in thought, Hope notices that and sits down next to them, they have very spiky and messy orange hair which has a bit at the front that goes down the middle of their face covering their nose, they also have glasses on as well as having bright red eyes, they have a gas mask on which is helping to cover most of their face, an earpiece in their left ear, under all that on the top half of their body, she is wearing a war style coat which looks like it could definitely take a few bullets, on her legs she's wearing some trousers made out of the same material on his feet, there are combat boots as well as gloves on both hands.

"Hey, you ok there?" Hope asks with concern in her voice.

The rebel makes a slight scream and jumps to the side before realising that it's Hope who just spoke to her.

"Oh, err...uhhh...." The rebel is unable to get any words out to Hope, she has a look of worry in her eyes, something was clearly playing on her mind, but what?

"Do you want to talk about it?" Hope asks in a calm voice.

Instead of saying anything, the rebel just shakes her head and gives Hope a hug.

Although caught off guard, Hope doesn't retaliate and hugs back.

"Hey, if you ever want to talk about anything, just come and find me." Hope says.

The rebel just nods, parts from the hug, pulls out a notepad and turns to a page with a script for what looks like a play.

Hope notices the stuff on the page.

"Did you write that?" She asks.

"Yes....it's shit isn't it?" The rebel asks in a quiet tone of voice but still loud enough for Hope to hear her.

"I haven't read it properly but from what I have read, it's not shit, you're a natural writer." Hope says, sounding extremely genuine.

"You...really think so?" The rebel asks.

"Yeah, have people been telling you that it's shit?" Hope says.

Instead of saying anything, the rebel nods and then points to a house on the other side of the road.

"I see, do you want me to do anything about it?" She asks.

The rebel shakes her head.

"Got it, can I mention something I've noticed about you, Gasmask?" Hope asks

Gasmask looks confused at Hope.

"When you're on missions or in combat you're extremely badass and confident but when you're here, you're very shy and have no confidence at all, do you want to talk about why that is?" Hope asks with concern in her voice

Gasmask takes some time to think before nodding her head.

"Alrighty, take your ti-" Before she can finish talking, Gasmask interrupts.

"Not...right now, maybe later." She says.

"Ok, got it, anyway I need to put this thing up on the corner of the building, do you think you'd be ok on your own?" Hope asks.

Gasmask nods, gets up then heads inside, meanwhile Hope puts the device on the edge of the base and goes in as well.

When she gets in, she is greeted by Henry and Megan.

"Done it, sorry it took so long, I was talking to Gasmask." Hope says.

"Hey, no worries, that's one of the things I respect about you Hockface, you like to check up on the rebels to see how they're doing." Henry says.

"Yeah, i'd much rather do that than pretend to know what they need/what and basically have a mutiny on our hands, anyway what do I do now?" She says.

"Just turn the TV on, open the guide then we should see so many more channels." Megan says.

Hope does that and just like Megan said, there are a ton more new channels.

"Perfect, that's phase one done." Suddenly an alarm goes off and upon hearing it, Hope and Megan run to a different room.

When they get to the other room, there are more rebels there, including Gasmask and the room looks like a briefing room with multiple tables set out in a partially square shape with an electronic whiteboard at the front of the room near the door, next to the whiteboard however are a bunch of post-it notes with different mission-related stuff on them and on the walls behind each rebel are a bunch of photos of rebels that are either MIA or have been KIA, on the wall is one that looks similar to Gasmask, except their hair is light red and they don't have a gas mask on the determined smile on their face is visible, however, there is a scar on the face of the person in the photograph but unlike some of the others, the person has been labelled as MIA.

Soon after, a person with light green hair, blue eyes a worried look on their face, and frog stickers also on their face, wearing a yellow hoodie with light blue jeans and trainers comes walking in along with a girl whose hair is a mix of blue and red, same shade of eyes as the person who is now up at the whiteboard as well as a red bowtie and a gothic tomboy style look complete with goth boots who sits down next to gasmask.

"So Hope, what's this I hear about you finally having a rebel codename?" The girl who just walked in asks.

"Yeah, I have one Gothboy." Hope says.

"Oooh, that sounds cool, what is it?" Gothboy asks

"Although temporary, it's hockface." Hope says.

"Cause of the hockey mask right?" Gothboy replies.

"Yep." She responds.

"Gotcha, hey I've gotta wonder, why do you a hockey mask over your face all the time?" Gothboy asks.

"I...don't want to talk about it." Hope responds.

"Awwww, come on, not even a little hint?" Gothboy replies.

"You're gonna keep asking that every time aren't you?" She responds with slight annoyance in her voice.

"Yep." She says.

Hope then sighs and then responds "Look, if we do this mission successfully and without a hitch then I'll show part of my face but not all of it, is that ok?" Hope asks.

"Ooooo, that sounds awesome." Gothboy replies.

Suddenly, the guy in the yellow hoodie starts talking.

"Errr....hi everyone, we're back here again because well, there's a new mission for you all, well some of you anyway, this mission just saying now is a mix between combat and stealth and is highly recommended that you go into two groups." The guy says

"However, that's only a recommendation." He continues.

"On here, I have how long it should take each team to do their portion of the mission." He says as the electronic whiteboard shows a page which says "Estimated times" on it, for the stealth team, there's an estimated time of about four hours and for the combat team, there's an estimated time of about 5 hours after everyone has noted the times down, the slide switches to the next one which says "Failure rate: 10% Equipment:".

"This mission, as you can see, has a 10% failure rate, it also has the list of equipment that is highly recommended for this mission." He says

"For the stealth team, you need to get the surveillance kit, a minibus from the garage at the end of this road and some explosives. For the combat team when it comes to the vehicles, you have free reign over what ones you use but please pick sensible ones." The guy says, looking at both Hope and Gothboy as he says that.

"What?" Hope and Gothboy say feigning ignorance

"I'm just going to pretend I didn't hear you two feign ignorance." He says.

"Anyway, as I was saying, the combat team have free reign of vehicles for this mission because well.....you have full permission to gun down or run over as many guards/soldiers as you all see fit." He says.

The eyes on all of the combat team's faces light up as if in sync.

"Well, does anyone have any questions?" He asks.

"Yeah, I have one" Gothboy says.

"Shoot." He responds.

"When you say any vehicle, do you include ones like the jet and helicopter?" She asks.

"Good question Gothboy and yes, those are included, however I don't recommend you use them BUT if you want to then that's up to you." He says.

"Sweeeeeeeeet" Gothboy responds.

"Any others?" The guy asks.

No one else asks any questions.

"Well, in that case, I hope to see you all return, you have a bit of time to prepare, I've marked the location for where the mission will take place on the Sat-nav of each vehicle so with that out of the way, good luck out there."

A few hours later, everyone on the combat team is gathered in the garage, all kitted up and ready to go.

"So, who's taking what?" Megan asks.

After hearing that, Hope sees probably the most ridiculous vehicle for a rebel combat mission ever, walks over to it, places a hand on it and says "If we put our minds to it, we can not only overthrow the king but...we can do it....IN A TRACTOR!!!!!" She says in a very enthusiastic tone while standing next to the tractor.

It looks brand new, however, it has very clearly been used before due to the mud tracks on the tyres. Despite that however it looked to be in perfect working order and upon seeing that, Hope gets in and attempts to turn the engine on but it overturns and refuses to turn on. Because of this, she gets out of the tractor while everyone else has unimpressed looks on their faces.

"Worth a shot though." She still has the same enthusiastic tone in her voice, clearly, she didn't regret it in the slightest.

Eventually, Hope just picks a suped up looking pickup truck which has had its cargo bed is prepared for eight rebels to sit on as well as the two in the cabin of the truck itself making an effective mode of transport for multiple rebels, Hope sits in the driver's seat of the truck while Gasmask sits in the passenger seat of the cabin.

The interior of the truck looks like it was recently cleaned out with the dashboard looking shiny and the seats having recently been replaced with brand new seats that look extremely pristine, once ready Hope puts her feet on the pedals but sits back waiting for the green light message to come through.

"Hey, Hockface?" Gasmask says quietly.

"Yeah, Gasmask?" Hope responds

"Do you think that after this mission...I could drive the truck back?" She asks

"I don't see why not Gasmask, especially if the stories I've heard are true." Hope responds.

"Wha- what stories?" She's taken aback by that and as such, has a surprised tone in her voice.

"Being an amazing *track racer* back when my parents ran the country." She says calmly while looking out the window.

"You knew about those...?" She asks.

"Yeah, I do like to perform background checks on rebels, it's to avoid any of the king's spies from getting in if he has any, although there's one thing I'm still confused about." She says.

"Huh?" Gasmask responds with a look of both confusion and worry in her eyes.

"I would ask but from what I can tell with your tone when at the base, you probably don't want to talk about it." Hope responds.

"Y...y...you mean the gasmask?" She says

"Yep." Hope responds.

"You're right...I don't want to talk about...yet." Gasmask says quietly as she looks down at the floor of the cabin.

"Combat team report in, combat team report in, over." The guy from before says on the other end.

"This is combat team four reporting in, over." Hope says

"This is combat team two reporting in, over." A different rebel from a different vehicle says.

However, there isn't any response from combat teams one and three.

"Combat teams one and three, do you copy?" The guy says

"Vetry, we have reason to believe that they may have gone on ahead." Hope says.

Vetry sighs, "Damnit, Gothboy is on one of those teams isn't she?" Vetry says.

"Actually no, Gothboy is on team two." Hope replies.

"That's weird, usually she's one of the first out of the gate." Vetry replies.

"I resent that!!!" Gothboy responds.

"You're not driving are you?" Vetry asks.

"Nope." She says.

"That explains it, anyway I need to inform all the teams that you now have clearance to go, stay safe and I'll see you all back here when you're done, over" Vetry says.

"Copy that, over." Hope says.

"Gotcha, over" The team two leader says.

After she finishes talking, Hope puts the key in the ignition, starts the truck, does a slight burnout and drives off outside the garage, followed by team two.

Soon after, both teams reach where the stealth team are, they are at a military base with no other personnel, however, due to the time that was due to change soon.

"Right combat team, should we brief you on what you all have to do?" Megan asks as both teams get out of their vehicles.

"If you want but before you do that, I have a question for literally any of the stealth team members." Hope says.

"Have any of you seen teams one and three somewhere?" She then asks.

All of the stealth teams just shake their head.

"Huh, weird, I just hope that they'll turn up soon."

"Right, mission briefing time: Because teams one and three aren't here yet, we may have to split you two up so just to stay on the safe side, let's go over positions; Team one, you'll be waiting right here at the gate, don't worry, you're not gonna be in plain sight straight away." Megan says.

"Once the king's soldiers arrive, you're gonna be throwing these grenades under their cars, now to minimise the chance of injury or death, I highly recommend that you run away literally the second you throw the grenades, like run while they're still in the air, once you see the explosion, pull out your guns and start firing at any alive and incoming soldiers." She says.

"Team two, you're going to be helping team three with this, your goal is to find the locations of the explosives that the stealth team planted, we would have activated them on our own and then be out of here by now but for some reason, Science Lab made them so that they can't be set off by the people who placed them, I don't know why, that's just how he did it." Megan continues

"Any questions so far?" She then asks.

"Yeah, for those looking for the bombs, would we be getting any indication for where they are?" Gothboy asks.

"Good question Gothboy and yeah you will, we drew schematics of the base as we were going around it and planting the explosives and placing little "x"'s in the area where they are, apologies in advance that they're not one hundred percent accurate and team four, you're going to be assisting team one on the frontline combat if all of this goes well then we should have this base levelled within the next four-five hours, any questions?" She then asks.

No response.

"Right, the soldiers should be back in ten minutes so we'll give teams one and three five minutes to show up and if they don't, then we'll split these two teams into two." Megan asks.

Five minutes later and it's still just teams two and four along with the stealth team at the gate.

"Right, it's been five minutes and the other two teams aren't here yet, so-" Just as Gothboy is about to continue, two more rebel vehicles turn up.

"I would ask why you're late but we don't have time, however, I will ask later." Megan says.

"For now, I just need to go over the plan again." She says, at that point, she goes over the plan while teams two and four get into the positions, soon after, team one is in their position.

The stealth team's minibus is also heard driving off.

One minute later, there's nothing but silence, until two explosions go off, at which point gunshots can be heard and soldiers are dying left, right and centre, meanwhile, teams two and four have split into multiple groups and are each searching for the explosives.

Gasmask however, has been left on her own so she goes into the shadows of the building, climbs onto the wall and starts moving across it, soon after she notices a soldier that somehow managed to get inside the building and as such, jumps down with very little noise, wraps one arm around the neck of the soldier, takes their gun and points it at their head.

"Give me one good reason why I shouldn't pull the trigger, you have ten seconds." She says in a much more darker and aggressive tone which is a vast contrast to her usual shyness.

"Do it, we know who you are..." A chuckle is heard coming from the soldier

"...Prove it!" Gasmask says.

"Ok then, how's this for proof?" The guard says as their voice is strained from the grip of Gasmask's arm.

"So..." Before the guard can finish saying the name, Gasmask shoots her gun into the soldier's head, let's the body drop and goes back into the shadows of the building.

In a different part of the building, Hope and Gothboy both hear the gunshot and continue walking down the dark hallway after stopping and inspecting to see if there are any soldiers nearby.

"Shit, do you think one of the soldiers got through the barricade?" Gothboy asks.

"Maybe but if they did then they still have to go through our resident assassin Gasmask." Hope says.

"Hockface, there's something I've noticed about you." Gothboy says while walking with Hope.

"What's that?" She asks.

"I'm not going to ask why but I've noticed that both you and Gasmask conceal your identities, nothing wrong with it, it's just been on my mind for a while now." Gothboy says.

Hope sighs.

"Gothboy, I trust you but you have to promise one thing.

"What's that?" She asks.

"If I show you my face then...you have to promise not to tell anyone who I really am because you'll know it straight away." She says.

"I promise, if there's one thing I respect from anyone, no matter what side they're on, is loyalty and unless you open up about this, I will take what you're about to show me to my grave." Gothboy says.

"..Thank you, shine your gun light on me please." Hope says as she takes off her mask.

"I...see, well, I can't lie I am shocked, however as I promised, I won't tell anyone this." She says as she turns around and pointing her gun light towards the route they're going, meanwhile, Hope is getting her mask back on.

After she has her mask back on, she catches up with Gothboy and finds the first two explosives.

"Right, so, how do we do this?" Gothboy asked.

She also shins her gun's torch onto the explosives each have a number pad and a warning stating that if it's moved then it'll explode on sight."

"Hmm, wait..." Hope notices something on the ground and puts it against the bomb, it's a keycard with her name on it and the screen on the bomb reads "WRONG PERSON, PLEASE TRY AGAIN, TWO MORE ATTEMPTS REMAINING!!!"

"Fuck but, why was this here then?" Hope asks.

"I don't know but I have my keycard on me, maybe we should try it?" Gothboy says.

"Yeah, may as well." Hope responds.

Gothboy puts her keycard against the bomb and it says "PERSON ACCEPTED, BOMB NOW ARMED, FIVE MORE TO GO!!!"

"Fuck...I really don't know if I want to show Hockface *that*." Gasmask says to herself while on a different end of the building, looking for the other explosives.

"I shouldn't be crying, not now, not ever, people like me don't have the right to cry." She says as tears are starting to form in her eyes.

Suddenly and out of nowhere, two armed guards appear from behind Gasmask and attempt to take her hostage.

"We got one of them, tell the alpha team that we got one of the rebels." One of the soldiers says.

Although her eyes are moist from the tears, that doesn't stop gasmask from flipping one of the soldiers in front of her, taking the gun then using that soldier as a hostage.

"You tell the Alpha team that was a mistake and you thought you had me but it was just a rat crawling around." Gasmask says.

"But, they're not going to fall for that." The soldier replies in a slightly panicked tone.

"I...don't...care." She says as she puts the barrel of the gun harder to the hostage's head.

"Do it, or I pull the trigger on both of you." Gasmask says.

The other soldier doesn't say anything.

After not hearing the other soldier not say anything, Gasmask pulls the trigger on the hostage and then immediately after, shoots the other guard square in the head.

After that, she goes back into the shadows and continues manoeuvring along the wall, after moving along the wall for an hour and not coming across any guards, Gasmask runs into a bomb that looks similar to the one that Gothboy and Hockface activated.

Upon seeing the bomb, Gasmask puts a finger on her earpiece and speaks.

"Guys, I think I found the bomb." She says

"What does it look like?" Hockface responds on the other end of the earpiece.

Gasmask replies with a description of the bomb.

"Perfect, that's it, there should be a keypad attached to the bomb" Hockface replies.

"Yeah there is, there's also a green, blue and red button respectively" Gasmask responds.

"Blue?" Gothboy says, sounding very surprised on the other end of the earpiece.

"Yeah, yours didn't have a blue one?" Gasmask asks.

"No, it didn't." Gothboy replies.

Suddenly, Henry cuts into the call.

"Hey, so I'll field this one: You see, each bomb is different slightly, however, they all have the same trigger sequence..." Henry explains the same procedure that Gothboy and Hockface used to activate their bomb.

"HOWEVER, these bombs are special in that unless ALL of them are triggered, their timers won't activate and as such, they won't explode so if you get captured by the guards before you can detonate them.....good luck." Henry leaves the call.

"Gasmask, listen to me carefully and input the numbers I say exactly." Hockface says.

"Got it Hockface." She replies.

"1 1 0 3 7" Hockface says.

Gasmask enters the numbers and then presses the red button as it lights up.

"0 0 0 1 1 7" Hockface says

She then enters those numbers then presses the green button as it lights up.

"L 1 0 0 1 5 R" Hockface says.

At first, Gasmask is confused then realises how to write letters so she then proceeds to write the code and presses the blue button as it lights up.

After doing that, a message on the bomb screen appears that says "BOMB ACTIVATED, FOUR MORE TO GO"

A few hours later, the bombs have been activated and each one says the same thing.

"TIME TO DETONATION: 5 MINUTES" Upon reading that, each rebel member who set off the bomb starts to make their way out of the base, most of the rebels were able to make it out; all except three:

Gothboy

Gasmask

Hockface

Those three rebels found themselves trapped inside the base with no way out and only two minutes left on the detonation.

"Shit." Gothboy said in a very worried tone.

Gasmask notices a keypad and presses codes, the same codes that were used for the bomb.

"CODE FAILED: TWO MORE ATTEMPTS BEFORE SELF DESTRUCT

Chapter 2: The King

A room filled with nothing, just pure blackness, no-one in sight, The King soon regains his composure.

"HELLO!!!!!" He bellows as loud as he can, not knowing that no-one can hear him.

"LUCA, IF THIS IS ONE OF YOUR PRANKS I'M NOT GONNA BE HAPPY" He bellows out again but still no response from anyone at all.

Instead of trying to get someone's attention, he just keeps walking onwards with the sound of footsteps echoing throughout the blank room.

'THUMP, THUMP, THUMP' The sound of The King's footsteps echoing.

'BATHUMP, BATHUMP, BATHUMP' The sound of his heart beating at a much louder volume.

Without warning, he hears another set of footsteps and looks around only to find...nothing there, he tries to look back the way he was going but because of the blank room, he can't figure it out and as such, starts walking in a different direction.

'THUNK, THUNK, THUNK' The sound of a second set of footsteps that are nearing him, however he turns around again and...nothing so he just continues walking but this time, taking things slowly and putting his right hand where his sword should be.

A creepy and childlike voice can be heard coming from somewhere.

"Circle you, circle you Children 'you just lost the game' circle you, circle you. Don't run away, you're the same, before the moon sets aside. Cut their neck off as they cried. Circle you, circle you. Who surrounds you everywhere?"

The voice just keeps repeating that over and over, after five loops, more join in then more, until there's ten voices that can be heard at which point, figures with empty eye sockets, bright white hair can be seen and all of them are each holding a replica of The King's sword, except every single one of them has blood on the edge of it and dripping off, making a drip sound as it hits the ground.

Alongside that, each sword also has a name and a number on it:

Aoife 15

Gordon 19

Sean 16

Matthew 20

Sophia 18

Megan 39

Lee 42

Alfie 50

Athena 45

Laura 51

Eventually each person and sword are all circling the king slowly while they repeat that line in a creepy and childlike manor, he tries to get up multiple times but is shoved down when each figure pushes him back to his knees, although their hands can't be seen, on their wrists a chain is just barely visible.

After the figures stop singing, the swords and the eyes just suddenly disappear and The King is able to get back up easily.

"IF I FIND OUT WHO DID THAT..." Before he could finish, a figure starts to speak.

"su ot sht dd oy" One of them said in the same creepy and childlike tone

"taf roy lla si sht" A second one said in the exact same tone.

After the second one stops speaking, the eyes disappear, no signs of anyone or anything anywhere until The King just collapses onto the ground.

Suddenly and without warning, the king wakes up with a cold sweat going down his body, he looks around his room to see that nothing has changed, it has a giant king sized bed against a wall at the back, the walls have a pitch black paint job, meanwhile the carpet has a checkered pattern on it and is coloured dark purple, the room is lit up by a chandelier which which is also showing the roof which is a vanilla colour.

After a few minutes of gaining his composure, the king gets off the bed, gets into his suit and leaves the room.

When he leaves the room, he is greeted by a dark and dreary hallway which has a marble floor with a black and white paint job, the grey sky coming in through the windows and no-one else there thus making a louding echoing sound every time the king walks in the room or when anyone else walks down the hallway.

The king walks down the hallway for a few minutes until he gets to a set of giant double doors at which point, he opens them then slams them as he walks into the throne room.

"SOLDIERS!!!" He shouts with a ton of dominance in his voice and as if on cue, three guards come running to the throne room and stand straight up facing the king while saluting.

"YES YOUR MAJESTY?!?" Each guard says in a disciplined manner.

"Today, I have a special mission for you." He says in response.

"I want you three to take some soldiers to this location." He pulls up a holographic map which shows the same base that the rebels are planning to destroy.

"I got wind that today, the rebels are planning to do something with this and as such I want you all to take some of our finest men to not only defend the place but also arrest some rebels and bring them to me directly and if any of you gets the rebel leader well then...Let's just say that there's a massive promotion heading your way." The king continues.

"So, any questions?" He asks.

"Yeah, one: What kinds of weapons will we get?" One of the soldiers asks.

"You'll all be using the same weapons that you have on you now, I trust that there are no objections?" the king says

Despite the soldiers clearly having objections, none of them say anything out of fear of what would happen.

"Oh one more thing: If any of you can catch that traitor and bring her here then you'll also be getting a massive promotion." The king continues.

"Well, that's all I'm telling you, get going now, I have urgent business to attend to." The king says and as such, the soldiers all leave the room.

A few hours later, when the king is sitting on his throne looking at the map which shows little dots which represents the soldiers, a hooded figure walks into the room.

"Greetings Your Majesty, I trust the intel I gave you came to fruition?" The figure says.

"Yes and don't worry, I didn't forget your payment." The king says as he gets up and heads to a secret vault near a corner of the room in the centre, after accessing the vault the king gets out a ton of money and hands it over to the hooded figure.

"I thank you, Your Majesty and if you ever need my services again, you know where to find me." The figure says as it leaves the room.

"Well, there is one more thing, I'll pay extra for it." The king says.

"Oh? And that is?" The figure says.

"You see this base on the map here?" The king goes over to the map and the hooded figure follows.

"Oh yes, Sidrer base, I know of the stories about it." The figure says.

"Well, I want you to go to that base and make it impossible for anyone to get in or out once the rebels you told me about are inside." The king says.

"Very well, I can do that but like I said, it's going to cost you extra, are you willing to pay for it?" The hooded figure responds.

"Yes I am, you know full well that I am good for it." The king responds.

"Very well, I expect half the payment now and half when I am done." The figure replies.

The king gets half of the needed money, hands it over and with that, the hooded figure leaves the room.

A few hours later, the hooded figure is sat outside of the base waiting and after a few hours of patience the rebels show up and go through their plans, suddenly one of the rebels catches the figure's attention, the one that suddenly grabs it's attention is Gasmask, however she doesn't notice the figure.

Soon after when the rebels and soldiers are in the building, the figure goes to the entrance of the base and locks it using a special code, after which it leaves the area and heads back to the castle.

The figure is back in the throne room.

"It is done, Your Majesty." The figure says while giving a bow.

"Very well and as promised, here's the other half of your cut." The king says as he gives the money to the figure.

"I thank you and if there's anything you need me to do, don't hesitate to get in contact." And with that, the figure leaves the room.

"That dream though...what could it mean?" The king asks himself quietly.

Instead of thinking too deeply into it, he looks on the map and notices that both the rebels and soldiers are stuck in the base and as such, the king presses a button.

"Soldiers, go out of the way you came, don't try to help the rebels." The king says while holding down the button.

After hearing that, the soldiers start running towards the area they came in and soon after they leave, the base explodes, however the because of the way the map is programmed, it doesn't show weather or not the rebels escaped, only the soldiers and a few hours later, each of the soldiers involved in the mission enter the throne room.

"I trust that the rebels have been killed if you don't have them?" The king says.

"That's what we think as well." One of the soldiers says.

"You...think?" The king says with his voice starting to become irritated.

"Well, they weren't with us when we escaped and they still weren't with us when the building went kaboom." A soldier says in a slightly worried tone.

"Well, go back and make sure that the Blood Renegades are dead then come back here as soon as you have confirmation." He says, raising his voice but not enough to be shouting.

"YESSIR!!!" The soldiers leave the room.

Soon after the soldiers arrive back at the base and explore it, they go to where the rebels were and find two things: A part of a bow tie and some orange hair.

"I don't know about you all but this to me confirms that they're dead." One of the soldiers says.

"Maybe but let's just look around to make sure." A different soldier replies.

After a few minutes of investigating, they find a bunch of fingers on the ground, each one looks as if they were recently detached from their bodies and still scorched from the explosion aftermath.

"Guys, what about these?" A soldier asks.

"I'd say that it does confirm their deaths then." A soldier says.

"Very well, if we're in agreement then we need to report back to the king with these fingers." A different one replies.

A bit later, the soldiers are back in the throne room with fingers, hair and a bowtie piece from the base explosion.

"And these are?" The king asks.

"Evidence that the rebels are dead." One of the soldiers says.

"So you can say with 100% certainty that they're dead?" The king asks.

"Yessir." All the soldiers reply.

"Good because if I find out that they're still alive then you know what will happen don't you?" The king asks in a threatening tone while gesturing to his sword."

"YESSIR!!!" Each soldier says with clear panic in their voices.

"Good, you're all dismissed." The king says.

With that, each guard leaves the room and three of them stay together.

"Hey guys." One of them says.

"Yeah Jacob?" Another one replies.

"Remember that pact we made about how we'd tell each other anything not tell anyone else?" Jacob says.

"Yeah?" A different one replies.

"Well I have something to tell you both but...I really need you two to honour the pact now more than ever." Jacob says, with clear nervousness in his voice.

"You know that we will Jacob." One of them says.

Jacob swallows.

"I've been thinking about trying to leave the royal soldiers and joining the Blood Renegades." Jacob says.

The other two soldiers are taken aback by this but don't leave the area.

"I respect that Jacob and I've just been wanting to leave the Royal Soldiers as a whole but can't." A different soldier says.

"Wow, I wasn't expecting that from you Alfie." The third soldier says.

"Yeah, how about you Riley?" Alfie asks.

"Me....I just want to pursue my dream." Riley says.

"This has just given me an idea..." Jacob says.

Riley and Alfie look at Jacob, clearly a confused look on their face.

"At some point within the next few days, we make a break for it and join the Blood Renegades." Jacob says.

"That's an ok plan but won't they shoot on sight if they see us, especially if we're approaching their base?" Riley asks.

"Maybe, however if we don't have the masks on and get a change of clothes then we can most likely get in without them knowing that we're ex soldiers." Jacob responds.

"True but how are we going to escape?" Alfie asks

"Hmmm, good question..."

Back in the throne room, the king is on a call with someone who is hiding their identity.

"Yes, everything is now in place for the plan to go ahead." The person says.

"Good, commence operation C" The king replies.

"Very well." Suddenly the throne room transformers into a security style room with monitors on every wall, monitoring every home in Edalbire.

"If you don't mind me asking, what exactly is your plan here?" The mysterious person asks.

"None of your business, your role in all of this is to just simply join them as a traitor, that's it, no more, no less." The king says.

"Very well then." The figure says.

"Firstly, before I even do anything, I want you to infiltrate the ranks of the Blood Renegades." The king says in a slightly determined tone

"And how would I go about doing that?" The figure replies.

"That's easy, just contact the number I'm sending you and he'll help you with the rest." The king says.

"Oh, I have something else for you to do while you're there." He continues.

"And that is?" The figure responds.

"Get Henry and bring him here, he will be very useful." He responds.

"I see and that leads me onto another question." The figure says.

"Yes?" The king responds

"How would I convince him to go to you?" It asks with confusion in it's voice.

"Easy, just say that he has an urgent message from the king, every citizen knows that when they have that, they have to legally attend otherwise they get executed." The king responds.

"I see, very well then, i'll get to it straight away." The figure replies.

"Good, I look forward to hearing back on your progress."

And with that, the communication cuts off.

A few nights later in the castle hallway.

"Have you checked every bedroom?" Alfie asks.

"Yeah, The King is fast asleep, he's a deep sleeper so we won't be able to wake him up." Jacob replies.

"Ah good, you two all set? Anything else you need before we commence operation escapation?" Riley asks.

The other two rouge soldiers feel their bodies and bags.

"Got everything." Jacob says

"Ditto." Alfie replies.

"Very well, let's leave this castle for good." Riley says determined.

"Ok, I'll lead because I installed all of the hidden traps so I know how to deactivate them temporarily." Jacob says.

"I've got no objections." Alfie replies.

"Same here." Says RIley.

The three soldiers make their way out of the hallway and into a grand dining hall which is lit up by a giant chandelier, in the middle of it is a long table going from one of the room to the other, next to the door on the other side exiting are two more soldiers standing guard, the floor also seems like it's made of marble, much like the previous room and each wall has been painted gold along with the floor.

"Right." Jacob whispers.

"We all go under the table, however there should be a keypad there, i'll press the buttons then that should deactivate the lasers." Jacob says.

"Very well." The other two say.

All three head under the table and when under it, Jacob notices the keypad, presses the combination that was set up then leaves from under it and walks to the door, however the other two soldiers stop them.

"HALT!" They both say.

"State your business." One of the soldier guards says.

"We need to speak to one of the prisoners." Riley says.

"State your codenames." The other soldier guarding says.

"Bounty." Jacob says.

"Storus." Alfie says.

"Vampire." Riley says.

"Ok then, you three can go on through." One of the guards says and both allow the three to leave the room through that door.

When they're through the door, they're greeted by another corridor which looks exactly like the one from before and to avoid suspicion from the two guards on the other side of the door they just left, they start walking in the direction of the prison.

Soon after, they get to the prison and enter it, it looks cold, damp and dreary with each prisoner looking at the three in fear, even after figuring out that they're not there for any of the prisoners, each cell however just has a metal bed, a dirty toilet and a sink inside them, with nowhere for privacy and each cell having a window that's barred up with mini bars to stop prisoners from trying to get out.

"Don't hurt me please." One says.

"I'll do anything you want." Another says.

The three however ignore them and head to a specific empty cell at the back of the cell rooms.

"Right, I'm assuming that you got everything ready in this cell?" Alfie asks Riley.

"Yep, the bars on the window should be loose, if we through these masks outside then we should be able to get out easily, however just know that it wasn't easy making the bars loose and we'd likely only get one chance at this so we better not fuck up." Riley responds.

"Got it." Both Jacob and Alfie say.

Alfie then proceeds to unlock the cell door with a key that he has and once done, all three enter the cell, at that point Riley grabs onto the bars and wiggles them loose, after around 10 seconds they come off at which point they slide the bar outside along with their mask and climbs out of the cell with relative ease.

Soon after, they hold their hand out to Jacob who grabs it and gets up using the same method then to Alfie who does the same.

Soon after, they're all outside on the castle grounds, however they still have a fair distance to go before they're free so they get their masks back on, hold their guns and start walking in a synchronised formation to avoid suspicion from any other soldiers.

The inside of the castle grounds is filled with dying plants, dark grass, a metal wall with a grey stone painting on it to make it look like an old stone castle from a distance.

Soon after, they notice that a wooden drawbridge connecting the castle to the entrance is present so Riley and Alfie look for a way to bring it down but Jacob stays standing where he is.

"That's not going to work, you two." Jacob says.

"Why not?" Riley asks.

"Look under it, I was ordered by the king a few years back to rig it to explode if someone tries to lower it as a way to keep out invaders." Jacob says.

"And you just did that?" Riley asks.

"I had no choice, if I didn't then you know what would have happened, hell right now all three of us are risking our lives." Jacob replies.

"Don't worry though, how are you two at swimming?" Jacob asks.

"I'm ok." Alfie responds.

"Same." Riley also responds.

"Sweet, we're gonna jump in the moat." Jacob says.

"And before you two say anything: Catch." He continues as he throws two gas masks to Riley and Alfie, once they have them, all three slightly lift up their usual masks and put the gas masks on.

"Ready?" Jacob asks.

Instead of saying anything, Riley and Alife nod.

"Ok then." Jacob jumps into the water, goes under it and down a hole that's been dug, at which point he's quickly followed by Riley and Alfie.

Chapter 3: Hope comes from a weird place doesn't it?

The three rebels were standing by the closed door, only a few minutes left on the timer and added onto that, only two more attempts before the place goes kaboom, before they attempt the second to last code attempt, they hear footsteps coming and as a response, Gothboy and Gasmask turn around and train their guns on the figures, however those three don't have their guns on them, instead they have their hands up.

"Don't shoot, we don't mean any harm." The middle one says in a panicked tone.

"Oh yeah? You have the masks that the King's guards wear, so sorry if we don't believe you." Gothboy says in a pissed off tone.

"Look, it's understandable if you don't believe us, however this might help you realise that we don't want to hurt you." After saying that, all three take off their masks and on the right is a young person, who looks around the same age as Gothboy, however under his dark red eyes, there are bags which indicates that the guard on the right hasn't had much sleep lately, not only that but the tone on their face reads as a pissed off 24/7 tone, alongside that his hair is short, spiky and dyed a mix of dark green and dark red.

"My name is Jacob." The one on the right says.

The guard in the middle is next to take their mask off is the middle one and unlike Jacob, they don't have any bags under their eyes, however there is a scar on the right side of their mouth, not only that but there is also a bandage flat where their nose should be and their hair is a natural blonde with it covering their left eye, their right eye however is clearly visible and is a hazel colour.

"I'm Alfie." The middle one responds.

The final guard takes off their mask and on their face is a determined look, however unlike the other two, they don't have any distinguishable features and seem sort of plain with the exception of their hair which is half neat and half messy plus dyed pink.
"And I'm RIley." The one on the left says.

"And we care about your names, why?" Gasmask asks in the same tone as Gothboy from before.
"Because we want to propose an alliance." Alife says.
"An...alliance?" Hockface responds in a confused tone.
"Yes, All six of us have a common interest: We all hate the king and how he's running things." Jacob responds.
"So, our offer is this: We join the Blood Renegades until your end goal is complete, which I'm assuming is to dethrone the king, correct?" He continues.
"You'd assume correctly, although we never really made it any secret that that's our end goal." Hockface replies.
"How can we trust you!!!" Gothboy says while snapping at the three guards.
"You five, we can't fight now, we're still on a timer." Hockface says.
Reluctantly, Gasmask and Gothboy put down their guns and the three guards put down their hands.
"If you want to get out, I know a secret way out that's only supposed to be accessible by the guards." Riley says.
"You sure? This isn't some sort of trap?" Gasmask asks.
"It's understandable that you're sceptical so I can't blame you for asking that, however right now, we don't have much choice, so lead the way you three." Hockface says.

"Not just yet, there is one more thing." Jacob says.

"Ooooooooooooooooooooofffffffffffffffffffffffff course there is, what is it?" Gothboy says.

"We need a little bit of Gasmask's hair, Gothboy's bowtie and Hockface's mask." Alfie says.

"Why so?" Gasmask asks in a sceptical tone.

"To make the king think that you three are dead when you're not." Riley says.

"So you want us to fake our deaths?" Gothboy asks.

"Pretty much." Alfie responds.

"And what do we gain?" Gothboy then asks.

"Short version: Three new allies who can become a major advantage for you as we have intel on The King's actions and his plan." Riley says.

"Oh? And how do we know you're not bluffing or just lying?" Gasmask asks.

"Guys, we don't have time for this, just show us the exit then you can explain yourselves later." Hockface says.

"Very well, follow us." Alfie says as the six of them run down a direction, meanwhile Gasmask and Gothboy are cutting a little bit of their hair and bowtie off respectively and Hockface pulling off a small bit of her mask revealing a tiny bit of her chin, once the six of them are out and on a nearby hill, they pass the stuff over to the guards and when they do that, the base explodes and the six flinch back.

"Well damn." The three rebels say at the same time.

"Right, now back to where we were before: How do we know you're not lying to us?" Gothboy says.

"Easy, see these tattoos?" All three guards pull down their sleeves which reveal three lion tattoos, all looking identical.

"Yeah? What about them?" Hockface asks.

"We aren't allowed to show them to anyone outside of the guards, they're a way to find out who really is one and who isn't and if you're disguising yourself as one and get found out then you face public execution." Jacob says, clearly with a sad tone in his voice, as if to imply that he's against the public executions that the king does.

"I see..." Gasmask says.

"Well, we'll see you later, we need to let the king know that you three 'died'" Alfie says that later with the "Died" being in air quotes and after that, the three guards run off towards the castle while the rebels run towards where the vehicles are.

A few minutes later, they get there and as soon as they arrive, the rebels that were waiting by the cars take a huge sigh of relief and they do it as if in sync.

"Well, some people are happy to see us." Gothboy says in a light hearted manner.

"Happy is an understatement, we thought you three died." A medium pitched spiky haired rebel says.

"Yeah, I can see how, sorry for making you worried." Hockface says.

"Well, we're just glad that you're safe." A different rebel says.

"Same here." Gasmask says.

"Should we all head back home now?" Hockface asks.

Nodding in agreement, everyone gets into the vehicles they arrived in and head back to the rebel base.

When they get back to the base, instead of heading in, Gasmask just sits down on the bonnet of the car and stares into space, very clearly distracted by something that's weighing on her mind, noticing that, Hockface sits on the bonnet of the same car next to her.

"Hey, you ok Gasmask?" She asks with worry in her voice.

"Wha- Y...y...yeah, I am." Gasmask says, she clearly didn't expect
Hockface to sit down next to her let alone speak to her, however the
way she said that, it's easy to tell that Gasmask is lying.

"You sure?" She asks calmly.

Gasmask doesn't respond and instead pulls out a photograph which
has three people in front of a car, all three look really happy, the
person on the left has hair that's similar to Gasmask, although instead
of it being orange, it's actually brown, the person's eyes however are the
same colour as Gasmask's and alongside having a happy smile, the
person is holding up a peace sign and is wearing a crop top plus jeans
and work boots, they also have oil on their face, however the person
doesn't seem to care.

Another person on the picture is someone that's slightly smaller than
the person on the left, however his hair is much more messier then the
person on the right's hair, his eyes are the same colour as the person on
the left, he also has the same clothes on as her, just a little smaller and
while the person on the left doesn't have anything in her hands, he has
a wrench in his hands and is also winking to the camera with an
innocent smile on his face.

The third person is crouching in the middle of the two, hugging both
of them as she also has a wholesome smile on her face, however unlike
the other two, it's impossible to tell what her eye colour is as her eyes
are closed, however she has very different clothes to the two as she's
wearing a suit as well as smart shoes, it's clear that the woman in the
middle was well off and unlike the other two in the picture, the
woman in the middle has fully neat hair and is clearly just as happy as
the other two people in the picture.

"This is an awesome picture, Gasmask." Hockface says.
"I'm guessing you know these people?" She then asks.
"...You could say that..." Gasmask says.
"I see..." Hockface says, knowing that Gasmask is hiding something.
"Would you mind if you say their names?" She then asks.
"The woman in the middle is Breanna, the boy on the right is Connor and the girl on the left is....So-Sapphire." Gasmask says with worry and sadness in her voice, it's clear that she's worried about the three.
"I just hope....Connor and Breanna are ok..." Gasmask says.
As soon as Gasmask says that, Hockface immediately puts two and two together and realises who 'Sapphire' is.
"I'm sure they are Gasmask and i'm sure they'd love to see Sapphire again soon, scratch that, i'm 100% sure that Sapphire will be able to see them again soon." Hockface says, clearly trying to comfort Gasmask.
"You...think so?" Gasmask asks.
"Yep." Hockface replies.
"It's a promise." Hockface says in a happy tone.
Out of nowhere Gasmask gives Hockface a hug and despite the suddenness of it, Hockface doesn't retaliate, instead she returns the hug.
"Thank you boss." Gasmask says.
"Gasmask, i've already said this but don't think of me as a boss, think of me as a friend because I think of you as a friend." Hockface says.
"Really...?" Gasmask asks.
"Mhmhm." She replies.
"...Thank you..." Gasmask replies.
"Anytime, oh and by the by, anytime you want to vent Gasmask, i'm here for you." Hockface says.
"Do you...really mean that?" She asks.

"Yep, and that's not just you, that's for every rebel, I don't like thinking of them as employees or me being their boss, I like to think of us as one big family and families look after each other."

No response from Gasmask, instead she's stifling a cry.

"Hey, if you want to cry, it's ok to let it out." Hockface says in a caring tone.

Instead of saying anything else, Gasmask just starts crying in the hug and instead of saying anything, Hockface just lets her cry.

A few hours later, Hockface is sitting down in the living room of the rebel base looking for a game to play that's downloaded on the game console connected to the TV when out of nowhere and without warning, Science Lab appears in the living room.

"Ah Hockface, just the person I was looking for, Gothboy and I need you downstairs in my lab." He says in a sort of excited but still trying to stay professional tone.

"Alrighty." Hockface puts the controller down and follows Science Lab down to his lab.

Soon after, the two are in the lab and Science lab takes Hockface to the vehicle that Gothboy is currently lying down on, taking a little nap, after noticing that, Science lab shakes Gothboy slightly and she wakes up.

"Ah Hockface, kinda got bored waiting for you." They say, not trying to hide the fact that they were napping.

"I thought so, anyway what do you need me for?" Hockface asks.

"Easy, just sit down on the vehicle that Gothboy was totally not napping on." Science lab says.

"OI! I WASN'T NAPPING, I WAS JUST.....resting my eyes" Gothboy exclaims.

"Yeah, yeah." As Science Lab says that, Hockface gets onto the ATV and turns on the keys which are in the ignition and some buttons on the vehicle light up.

"Right, first thing I want you to do..." Science lab stands in a giant circle in an open area of the lab.

"Ride the ATV towards me and don't brake." He says, plus hearing that shocks Hockface.

"You sure Science lab?" Hockface asks with a slightly scared tone in her voice.

"Yep, trust me on this." He says.

As such, she reluctantly drives the vehicle towards Science Lab who doesn't flinch and then out of nowhere, something comes up on a screen on the handle bar which reads 'ALLY LOCATED' and as such, comes to a stop right before it can make contact with him.

"See what I mean?" He asks.

"Damn, that's cool." She exclaims.

"Try and drive it again." He says.

She tries to but it doesn't move and the engine just revs with the screen saying 'ATV WON'T MOVE UNTIL ALLY IN FRONT HAS MOVED' After that appears, she stops revving the engine then sits up on the ATV.

"O-o-o-o-o-o-o, can I explain the big red button?" Gothboy asks.

"It's not big but yeah, it's a red button and go for it Gothboy." Science lab says as he and Hockface move the ATV back to where it was.

"RIGHT, EVERYONE, CLEAR THE AREA....AKA, GET WHAT YOU NEED AND GO BEHIND ME!!!" Gothboy shouts and as she does shout that, people grab what they need and head behind her, at that point a bunch of walls also appear from under the floor including one right infront of Hockface, Science Lab and the ATV, although that wall has a special sized hole, despite that though, it's possible to see inside the walls from where everyone is.

"So Hockface, do you want the short or long explanation?" Gothboy asks.

"Errr, both?" She responds.

"Short: Button + being pressed + Giant gun behind you = Explody in front of you." Gothboy says with a smirk on her face.

"Long: When your brain gives your arms the command to move and your hands to..." Hockface interrupts Gothboy.

"I take back the long thing." She says.

"You know what, fair, I was gonna go all scientific on your ass." Gothboy replies in a light hearted tone.

"So when you're ready, press the red button." Gothboy says.

Hockface presses the button after which a missile fires from above and behind and hits the target inside the walls and not only does the explosion go off without a hitch, Gothboy looks at it with awe as it stays within the walls with no damage to the walls taken, after the explosion clears the walls go down and a few small fires from the area are soon clear at which point, people start going back to their workstations and continues working on the experiments.

"Right, press the green button, that should be next to the red button, press it." Science lab says as Hockface does press the button.

"Eh? What's supposed to happen?" She asks in confusion.

"Perfect, it worked." Science Lab exclaims.

"Eh?" Sound of confusion from Hockface.

"Oh right, you can still see yourself and the vehicle, however we can't, in short, you're invisible to everyone except yourself because of that." He explains.

"What's better is that you can combine that with the missile button so enemies won't know where the missile came from and KABOOOM!!!!" Gothboy says excitedly.

"Noice." Hockface says.

"I'm assuming that to deactivate it, I just press the button again?" Hockface asks.

"Yep." He replies.

She presses the button again and now becomes visible to all those around her.

"Right, final button: The blue button, i'll just explain what it does because It's still not 100% yet." Science lab explains.

"Ok then." Hockface says as she gets off the ATV and goes to where Science Lab and Gothboy are standing.

"Right, have you played MK8?" He asks.

"Not really but I have seen footage of it." She says.

"Close enough, so you're aware of the anti-gravity feature in the game right?" He asks.

"Yep." She replies.

"Well, that blue button basically activates anti-gravity and while it is based off the MK8 version, it isn't entirely 100% like that, in short, the intention with it is to allow the ATV to travel on all sorts of angles on buildings and walls, however that doesn't work as planned just yet because while it does go up them, without pressing the button again or crashing, it's near impossible to put it back on the ground; what we plan to do with it is to give it the same transition from ground to wall and wall to ground and vice versa." Science Lab explains.

"I see, well, do you have an approximate date for when it'll be done?" Hockface asks.

"Not yet, but I am hoping that it'll hopefully be completely finished by the end of the month." He says.

"But, that's tomorrow." Hope says in a worried tone.

"It is?" Science Lab checks the date while saying that.

"Shit, I didn't realise, well time does fly when you're focused or having fun." He says.

"Science lab, you don't have to set yourself a deadline, it's perfectly ok to take as long as you need, we're nowhere near ready to storm the castle yet, we've still got a hell of a lot of preparing to do." Hockface says.

"I know, I just like setting deadlines for myself as it helps motivate me and give me A reason to actually do stuff.

"I see, well that's understandable, just keep that in mind for the future." She says.

"Will do....Hockface, can I ask you something real quick?" He says.

"Sure, anything Science Lab." She responds.

"What gifts would you recommend getting for someone you love who's birthday is coming up?" He asks.

"Well, the best thing I'd say is just get them something that you know they'd like, or at the very least appreciate, or you could also make something for them, it's entirely up to you." She says.

"I...see..." Science lab seems weirdly deep in thought.

"Hmmm....I know." His face lights up and he runs out of the lab.

A few minutes later, Science lab comes running back into the lab.

"Right, that's that taken care of, now follow me Hockface, there's a little gadget I want to show you." He says as he and Hockface walk down to a different area of the laboratory and he shows a small green cube with an electric effect coming out of it.

"This little toy, I don't have a name for yet-" Gothboy interrupts.

"The electro-cube." They say.

"The electro-cube is something I think you're all gonna enjoy, I say that cause we plan to mass produce it to have enough for around two for every rebel." Science lab says.

"Not only that but this thing has the ability to disable the electronics of the room it's in if it's thrown AND added onto that it also can temporarily paralyse anyone in it's range, so if you do use it, I don't recommend aiming it where some rebels are unless you have absolutely no choice when in the raid or on a mission.

"I see, I don't need to test it because I can picture in my mind just how it'll work." Hockface says

"I wasn't gonna let you test it anyway because of the risk of paralysing people here, however I can confirm that it does work." Science lab says.

"Ok, can't blame you." Hockface replies.

"So, do you need me for anything else?" She asks.

"Nope, i'll see you later." Science lab says as he goes back to the ATV and opens up the seat on it and starts work on it, meanwhile Hockface leaves the lab.

After Hockface and Gothboy have left the lab, Vetry walks into it and goes up to Science Lab.

"Heya." They say as they hug from behind.

"Damnit Vetry, I wasn't expecting you for another hour, also you're lucky that you're the only one who can hug me while I'm in my lab clothes." He says.

"Hehe, sorry, I'm just done with everything I had to do for today and wanted to see how my amazing boyfriend is doing." Vetry kisses Science Lab on the cheek after they say that.

"I guess you're gonna take another hour then?" They ask.

"Yep, at the least." Science lab responds.

"Very well, i'll speak to you later then." Vetry says, after that they give Science lab another kiss on the cheek then walk out of the room. Science lab then sighs and looks down at the little robot they're holding.

"Do you think I give them too hard a time sometimes? All they want is for me to love them and I do love them back but I feel like i'm sometimes too hard on them, especially since in the rebels, they have a much easier job, what do you think Proto?" He asks.

"Beeep beep beeeeep." Proto responds.

"You too huh?" He says in response.

The robot jumps out of Science lab's hands and onto a nearby desk, it is designed so that it looks slightly humanoid but mainly robotic, It has a digital face that can and does change depending on the emotions that either the person is holding is feeling or based on the context of the situation, the digital face right now is a worried/concerned look and the colour of the face is purple.

"Beep, beep, beeeeeeeep, beep..." Proto says in a worried tone.

"Yeah, I'm ok, just kinda...thinking." He responds.

"Beep?" Proto says in a confused tone.

"About Vetry and the rebels as a whole, like...is making stuff for others really all that i'm good for? I just feel like I might be able to do more and yet...I can't..." Science lab says again, but this time, he almost sounds like he's in tears.

"I'm just a fucking weakling who can't do anything else." He says, still almost sounding like he's in tears.

"I know people say i'm strong, but i'm fucking not, all i'm fucking good for is making stuff and once the rebels goals are complete, everyone's just gonna fucking abandon me." He continues.

Soon after, Science lab has burst into tears and has now started crying.Proto is there trying to help the other people in the lab provide comfort to him.

Back in the living room, Hockface is looking through some plans on the table with 'Receive and Slash You' playing on a nearby radio, while looking through the plans, she hears a knock at the door but before she can answer it, Megan does instead.

"Hello?" She says.

"Oh? Is this the right place? We did get it right, right?" A familiar voice to Hockface says.

"Who are you three?" Megan asks.

"Jacob, Alife and Riley." One of the three says.

"We're here to join the Blood Renegades." Alfie says.

"Ooo, alrighty, let me just quickly get our leader..." Megan says before Hockface interrupts.

"Megan, I already said, don't think of me as a leader, think of me as a friend." Hockface says.

"Hehe, sorry Hockface." Megan replies as hockface walks to the door. When she gets there, she notices the three.

"Ah, I was starting to think you weren't gonna show up." She says.

"You know them?" Megan asks.

"Yeah, me, Gothboy and Gasmask ran into them when we were trapped inside the base, hell if it wasn't for these three then we'd be dead right now." Hockface replies.

"WAIT, YOU ALMOST DIED?!?!?!" Megan shouts in a very surprised tone.

"It's not the first time it's happened." Hockface says casually.

"I know but if these three weren't there, you would have actually died." Megan replies.

"Yeah, that's true, so you three wanna come in?" Hockface asks as they move to the side to let the three through.

"Oh? Sure." All three walk in and Hockface guides them to the living room.

"Just take a seat." Hockface says as she sits down on a couch."

"Righto, before we can let you in, you three do need to pass a training course to make sure you're athletic enough to go on missions should you want to, if you wish to take part in the other stuff then just let me know and I'll get the leader of that specific team for ya." Hockface says.

"Well, actually...I would like to help out with strategising rather than field stuff if that's ok." Alife replies.

"That's fine with me, how about you two?" Hockface asks.

"I wouldn't mind helping out in the field." Riley responds.

"I don't have any preference, I'd be happy to help wherever I can."
Jacob responds.

"Very well, in that case; I'll quickly get Vetry up here to teach Alfie
about the strategizing stuff, I'm sure that they'll appreciate the extra
help." Hockface says.

She gets the walkie-talkie that's on the table and speaks into it.

"Vetry, you're needed in the living room." She says.

"Got it, I'll be up in a few minutes." Vetry responds.

"Thank you." She says, after which she puts it back on the table.

"Right, Riley and Jacob, just go down the hallway, turn left, left again
then right and through the first door on the right, you should see the
course, I'll meet you two there, I just need to explain to Vetry what's
going on." Hockface says.

"Got it." The two say as they get up and go the direction that
Hockface told them.

A few minutes later, Vetry appears in the living room.

"You wanted to see me Hockface?" They ask.

"Yeah, there's someone here who is interested in becoming a mission
strategist." She responds.

"Oh, sweet, I'd love the extra help, I'm guessing it's the person sitting
on the couch?" Vetry asks.

"Yep, why don't you two introduce yourselves to each other, I need to
go check on something else." Hockface says as she leaves the room.

"Alrighty, so what's your name?" Vetry asks.

"Alfie, i'm assume that you're Vetry?" Alfie responds.

"Yep, so before we begin, what expressed your interest in becoming a
strategist for missions?" Vetry asks.

"Well, it's a long story and well....I'm ashamed about most of it and
don't want to talk about it." They respond.

"I understand 100%, is there anything from it that you do want to mention though?" Vetry asks.

"Oh yeah, there is one thing: I've always loved making plans, planning things out and just seeing those plans executed either by myself or by someone else." They reply.

"That's wonderful, there's nothing better than a plan that comes together and works perfectly." Vetry responds.

"Agreed 100%." Alfie gets a twinkle in their eyes, it's clear to Vetry that this is something that they are passionate about.

"Oh, before we go any further, I must ask: What are your pronouns?" Vetry asks.

"Uhhhhhhhhhhhhhhhhhhhhhhhhhhhhhhhhhhhhhh.......ERROR, PRONOUNS NOT FOUND, PLEASE REBOOT SYSTEM ALFIE.EXE." Alfie responds in a robotic voice along with very clear comedic intent and as such, Vetry is trying their best not to laugh.

"Joking aside though, if I were to say then I'd probably say they/them, how about yours?" Alife says with a smile on their face.

After a few seconds, Vetry manages to calm and responds.

"They/them as well, although sometimes I go by she/her but I prefer the former." They respond.

"Got it and I'll make sure to respect that." Alfie responds.

"Awesome, so should I show you to the strategy room?" Vetry asks.

"Lead the way." Alfie says as the two stand up and walk out of the room.

A few minutes later, they both get to the mission strategy room, the room looks similar to the briefing room, except there's a holographic map in the middle of it and what looks to be mini monitors and a keyboard on the sides of it, the walls of the room are decorated with non binary flags and one end of the wall having the colours painted on, after seeing that, Alfie's eyes light up in pure joy.

"I guess you like it then?" Vetry asks happily.

"I love it Vetry." Alfie responds.

After that, Vetry walks over to the giant computer in the middle of the room, presses a few buttons and a holograph of the map of Edalbire.

"Vetry, why do you have a map of the country up?" Alfie asks.

"Simple, just select a random area on the map, it doesn't matter whereabouts." Vetry says.

Alfie walks up to the holographic map.

"You sure Vetry?" They ask.

"Yeah I am, just zoom in like this:" Vetry stretches their arms out and moves them in to zoom the map in and moves them out to zoom the map out.

"Coooooool, I still find it mind boggling how far technology has come." Alfie says.

"Same to be honest." Vetry replies.

After that, Alfie zooms in on a random piece of farmland.

"You're a natural Alfie, next, select 'confirm' or 'deny', after which choose a bunch of names then press 'confirm'." Vetry says.

Alfie does what Vetry said and as such selects a bunch of names: 'Hockface', 'Gasmask', 'Gothboy', 'Bookworm', 'Ace Attorney', 'Hope' and 'Despair'. After each name is selected, Gothboy presses 'Confirm'.

"Right, that's part one done." Vetry says.

"Next, we need to figure out what the rebels you selected need to do on this makeshift mission." Vetry says.

"So, we have multiple choices here: A: This could be a stealth mission and as such, it may be better to swap Gothboy for someone else cause well, she's not exactly the most stealthiest rebel." They continue.

"B: It could be an all hands on deck mission which basically needs everyone's expertise." They continue.

"C: It could also be a breaking and entering mission and if that's the case then depending on the type of breaking and entering; it may be a good idea to swap either Gasmask out or Gothboy out, if you want it done quietly then keep Gasmask and swap Gothboy, the opposite is true for if you want it loud and explody." They continue.

"D: It's also possible to select only one rebel to send out on a solo mission should that be needed." Vetry says.

"I have a question about D." Alfie responds.

"Go on." Vetry responds.

"With that one, are they usually missions that cater to one specific rebel's talents/roles?" Alfie asks.

"Pretty much, so for example..." Vetry takes the menu back a few and selects just Gothboy.

"If we were to just send Gothboy on a mission alone then we'd get a list of missions in the general area we're in that cater to her specialty, namely missions that involve being loud and having alot of explosions." Vetry continues.

"It applies to any of the rebels should you need to send them out on a solo mission so Hockface won't get the same solo missions that Gothboy has." They continue.

"Any more questions?" They ask.

"Actually, one: Does something similar apply if I select two rebels on a mission?" Alfie asks.

Vetry puts his hands together as a sort of clapping motion but instead of actually clapping, they just keep their hands together.

"I'm glad you asked Alfie because you see, something similar does apply but it is quite unique if I do say so myself." They respond.

"Oh? How so?" Alfie asks.

"Excuse me one moment, I've always wanted to do this." Vetry quickly leaves the room then comes back in a steampunk Sherlock Holmes inspired outfit.

"It's elementary my dear enby friend, for you see, should you select two rebels then you'll get a list of missions which easily fit into the skillset of the two rebels selected, so for example should there be a mission that requires two people and both stealth and loud explody entrances then Gothboy and Gasmask would be your best bet, or if there's one that requires precision melee attacking and careful onsight planning then Samurai and Hockface would be your best bet." Vetry responds.

"Sweet, what else do I need to know?" Alfie asks.

"I'm also glad you asked that, for you see, you can also assign times to certain missions and predicted foot traffic around the area at said times so you can work out the best times for the missions to be assigned and completed, we usually try to time them for the least amount of foot traffic." Vetry responds

"Ah, I can understand that." Alfie responds.

"Is there anything else I need to know?" They then ask.

"Actually there is one thing, incase a rebel is unavailable for any reason, say ill or dead...god, I didn't mean to go so morbid, anyway incase they're unavailable just swipe a rebel's name left then you'll get a choice, if it's temporary then select the top one and if you go back into the rebel list then you won't see their name in the list, however sh could it be a more permanent reason as to why they can't, such as being killed or leaving the rebellion then do the same thing as before but press the bottom one, any questions?" Vetry responds.

"Yeah, one actually: How do I put a temporary rebel back?" Alfie asks.

"That's easy, just go to the main menu, press 'Out of Commission rebels' then press the one who can be sent into missions again, should they change to a more permanent reason as to not being able to attend missions then press the bottom button on the menu that pops up, same applies for putting back but replace bottom button with top button." Vetry responds.

"Alrighty, anything else I need to know about it?" Alfie asks.

"Right now; no, however there is more to come later on and when needed I'll tell you about it but right now, what I've told you is all you need to know." Vetry responds.

Hockface, Jacob and Riley are all standing in a locker room but none of them are in their usual outfits, instead they are in training gear which consists of a tactical bulletproof vest, that is in front of a plain white shirt, tracksuit bottoms in the which has a dark green colour scheme as well as having a pocket on them which fits the pistol that's inside them, along with combat boots on the feet of all three and a dark helmet, Hockface's visor is down while the visor's for Jacob and Riley are still up.

"Ready to begin your combat training?" Hockface asks.
"Yep." The other two say.
"Right, set your helmets to training mode instead of combat mode, just so that if you accidentally shoot each other, it'll only sting a bit and not actually injure or kill you, to do so just press the button on the side of your helmet and on the menu, press the 'Combat mode' button." Hockface says.
The two do that and once done, the three enter the training field.

Once they get there, they are greeted with what looks to be a barren wasteland with the exception of a few seemingly red explodey barrels, after noticing that, Jacob aims at one of them.
"Go on, shoot it, see what happens." Hockface teases.
"Are you challenging me? The champion of shooting red barrels." Jacob asks in a teasing tone.
"Hmmmmmm.....maybe." Hockface says in the same tone.
In response, Hockface signals to someone in the room on the top and they spawn in multiple red barrels.
"An attempt to make the training more fun, all three of us take turns and whoever shoots the most wins, not only will this help with

friendly competition since sometimes people here take part in friendly competitions for each other." Hockface says.

"Ooo, sounds fun, how many points do we need to win?" Riley responds.

"Hmmm, there's three barrels, I would probably say first to thirty points wins." Hockface replies.

"You're on." They both reply.

"Sweet, a few ground rules first:

A: No shooting each other.

B: Only shooting the red barrels.

And

C: Have fun." Hockface says.

"Just one question before we start." Riley says.

"What happens if we shoot each other?" He continues.

"Easy, you lose twenty points." Hockface says.

"Got it." Riley replies.

"Ready?" Hockface asks.

"Mhmhm." The two say as they aim their guns at the barrels.

Hockface aims her gun at the barrel.

"FIRE!"

All three fire their weapons at the barrels, while they don't explode officially, they do make an explosion visual effect to simulate an explosion, it doesn't stop them from shooting and after ten minutes all three stop shooting and a screen appears with the numbers and names shuffling.

"That was fun." Riley says.

"Agreed." Both Jacob and Hockface respond.

"So, what's next?" Riley asks.

"Well, you both are natural shooters, hell all three of our scores were tied at 30." She says.

"Heh, thanks." Both RIley and Jacob respond while blushing lightly.

"And because of that, I don't feel like you two need to continue with the training since it seems like you've had some already." Hockface says.

"Yeah, when we were made to join the guards against our wills, we kinda had no choice but to do so." Riley responds.

"Damn...that sucks, well here in the BR, you won't have to do anything you don't want to do, we want everyone to be comfy, happy and if you ever want to talk about anything or just have a chat then usually people won't mind that." She continues.

"Really?" Jacob asks.

"Yep." Hockface says in a happy tone.

"Do either of you two have any questions?" She then asks.

"Actually, I do have one: What does BR stand for?" Riley asks.

"Blood Renegades." Hockface says.

"Or if that's too violent, just call us 'Rebels', I usually try to go between both." Hockface responds.

"Anymore questions?" Hockface asks as all three of them put their guns back to where they got them from.

"None from me." Riley says.

"Same here." Jacob says as well.

"Ok then, well, I'll see you back upstairs if you want to stay down here for a bit longer to practice." She replies.

"I'll come with you, I don't really feel like doing much right now." Riley says.

"Same." Jacob responds.

Once the armour is off and the guns are put back, all three make their way back to the living room.

Once they get there, they see that Vetry and Alfie are already there, bonding and having a laugh.

"I see you two get along really well." Hockface says.

"Yep, we've got a surprising amount in common." Alfie says.

"Well, I'm glad that you two have become fast friends." Hockface responds.

"Same, so how did your field training go?" Vetry asks.

"Really well, these two here are natural shooters and our scores were super close....well, ok they were tied." Hockface says.

"Waitwaitwaitwaitwaitwait, back up the truck....did ALL THREE of you get 30?" Vetry asks in surprise and as a response, all three nod.

"Damn, I've never seen anyone get close to Hockface's score let alone tie it." Vetry says, still in the same surprised tone.

"So how did things go with you two?" Hockface asks.

"Really well, I learnt so much and also became friends with them." Alfie replies.

"Niceeeeeeee." Jacob responds.

A few hours later, in the living room Gasmask is napping, Gothboy is playing a game and the alarm....it starts to go off and that gets the attention of the two at which point, they jump up and head to the mission briefing room.

Once there, only two other rebels are already there: Vetry and Alfie.

"Ah, welcome you two, we just need to wait for the others then we'll be all set."

"Very well then..." The two take their seats, It's clear that they don't trust the three newest rebels at all and with very good reason.

Soon after, the other rebels start coming in one by one and then they take their seats.

"Welcome, we have a new mission for you today but first before that, we also have three new rebels with us, however there isn't any time for introductions right now." Vetry says.

"The mission today is one that I feel like some of you might hate but is one that we're gonna have to get out of the way before we can begin with the big operation." They continue.

"Yep and for this mission, you're gonna be split off into multiple teams, the more stealthier rebels are gonna be on one team, the more frontward attack rebels are gonna be on another team and so one....basically, the teams you're in are focused on your abilities, this is to make sure that we get the best result from the mission." Alfie says.

"Mhmhm, So get into your teams now and we'll explain what each team is doing after you've done that." Vetry responds.

After a few minutes, all the rebels are in their respective teams and are standing in their teams, although some are sitting.

"Sweet." Vetry brings up a holographic map of the country then zooms into one area.

"Firstly, the assassin team: You all are going to have your assassination skills tested as there's a few high profile people on the King's side that you all need to take out, I would recommend going multiple per person, however the way you do it is completely up to you all so I would recommend talking about it amongst yourselves before you actually start." Vetry says.

"Secondly, the breaking in team." Alfie zooms into another area on the map that's nearby.

"You all need to break into this building here, inside this building are vital documents that you all need to collect, if memory serves, they should be secret documents that the king hid there explaining where all the weak points on the castle are and the best places to storm it, judging by context and what i've been told by Vetry here, it seems to me that, that's gonna be some very important information and very beneficial." Alfie says.

"However there is a reason why we've assigned you lot to this: The place is supposed to be heavily guarded and sneaking in is not a viable option so the best result is a straight head on attack to the guards." They continue.

"Yep, however don't worry because you'll be heavily armoured even though you won't look it because Science Lab has perfected the new armour and it's waiting for you all down in the armoury, that applies to all the teams by the way should you choose to wear it." Vetry says.

"So those bastards won't stand a chance." Alfie then responds in a determined tone.

"Finally, we have the assault team." Vetry then zooms into a third part of the map as they say that.

"Your mission is to raid this secret base which is yet again, run by the king, however while this one isn't heavily guarded, it still is guarded and the armour is highly recommended." They continue.

"Inside the base however, is a prototype weapon that the king has been working on, I don't know exactly where it is but I do know the general location of the weapon." Alfie says as they zoom in to a specific part of the base and draw a circle over two rooms.

"It should be in one of these two rooms, however if it's not, make sure to check every room." They say.

"Any questions?" Vetry replies.

"Yeah, I have one." An unnamed rebel responds.

"Yeah?" Vetry responds."

"How does the other person know all this? Are they a spy or something?" The same rebel asks and after which sounds of agreement can be heard coming from the other rebels...except for three: Gothboy, Gasmask and Hockface as those three already know the truth behind why Alfie is there.

"Guys, please be quiet." Hockface says with her voice raised.

"I'll field that one after the mission, if that's ok." She says.

Vetry and Alfie both nod in response.

No responses from the other rebels.

"Any other questions?" Vetry asks.

Just silence which indicates that no-one has any more questions.

"Very well, if no-one has anymore then that's the briefing over so go and get ready and I'll hopefully see you all later."

In the locker room, each team are in the armour that was worn by Jacob and Riley during the training, although the assassin team aren't wearing them, instead they just stick in the clothes they are currently wearing.

Once changed, Gothboy walks up to both Jacob and Riley.

"Just know that I don't trust you." She says quietly to the two.

"We understand, however we'll do everything we can to get you to trust us because we do genuinely hate The King." Riley says.

"Gothboy, a word?" Hockface says as she takes Gothboy to a corner of the room.

"Look, I get that you don't trust them, hell I'm neutral on the two myself but please don't let that compromise the mission, this may be the only chance we get to get secret intel on The King, his weapons and it could also be the final thing we need before the big operation." Hockface says.

"I know Hockface, it's just that...they used to be guards and if life has taught me one thing repeatedly...it's that someone evil never changes to good." Gothboy says.

"Yeah that may be the case, however if what they said is true then they were never evil in the first place." Hockface says.

"Just...forced into a situation they couldn't get out of until now." She continues.

Gothboy sighs.

"I trust your judgement on this Hockface so for your sake and the sake of the BR, I hope you're right." Gothboy responds.

All three teams leave the building and head in the directions that they needed to go in, the breaking in team head towards the base which Vetry and Alfie mention, the trip takes them through a few small towns and ends in the middle of the forest.

"Guys...we sure this is the right place?" One rebel asks.

Hockface pulls out her binoculars and sees a base in the distance, camouflaged by the trees.

"Yep, a bit ahead, sneaky bastards though, they somehow managed to camouflage it behind the trees." Hockface responds.

"WHAT THE- HOW?!?!?!" A different rebel responds.

"Not sure, we may find out when we get that and we may not, despite that though..." She turns to the rebels.

"Don't forget what we're here for, we're here to break into that base, find the secret weapon documents, maybe find other secret stuff then get the hell out of there." Hockface says.

"So we have two choices A: Sneak in and avoid all the guards or B: Head on attack." She continues.

"Who here wants to do option A?" As she asks that, half of the rebels put their hands up.

"Ok, that leaves the other half for option B, so let's flip a coin, heads for option A and tails for option B, is that ok with everyone?" Hockface asks.

Everyone nods and in response, she gets out a coin and flings it up in the air as it spins round many times, when it gets low enough, she catches the coin on her hand by covering it then lifts it up to reveal heads.

"Ok then, looks like we're sneaking in, that being said however, if you can do it stealthily feel free to kill a guard." Hockface says.

"Because it's the stealthy approach though, it'll be best to go about this on foot rather than using the car." Hockface says.

As soon as Hockface finishes saying that, her and the rebels start walking towards the base, however once they get close enough they stop walking normally and instead start sneaking towards it.
"Right, it may be best if we split up, half of you take the other side and we'll take this side, also should you want to kill a guard, make sure your guns have their silencer activated/turned on or you know how to do it via hand combat." Hockface says.
"Mhm." Half of the rebels go round to the other side of the base, the main base itself right now is covered by a giant wall so they can't see inside it so they have no idea how it looks inside, despite that though, thanks to the briefing however, the breaking in team do have an idea of the layout of the base so they're able to work from that.
Soon after scanning, they find a little crack in the wall.
"Hmm...Well, we could use explosives to get through but that should probably only be if we can't find anything else, however that would immediately alert them to our presence, despite that however, we do need to keep it as an option." Hockface says.
Each rebel nods in acknowledgement.

Before they can continue sneaking around, they hear an alarm go off.
"Shit, it looks like they know that we're here." One of the rebels responds.
"True, guys get your guns ready, we're probably about to face a bloodbath here." Hockface responds as she gets her assault rifle off her back.
Each rebel does the same and they all run around to the front of the base where the rebels that accidentally set off the alarm.

However once they get there, not only are they greeted with the front of the base which looks similar to the one they raided before just with a different colour scheme.

However, just as they start to get ready to fire, the other team notices that the guards that were outside are now dead and none of the rebels have died.

"Damn guys, I'm impressed." Hockface responds.

"Thanks but there's likely more on their way as we speak." Jacob responds.

"Good point, let's get in there, find those documents, find anything else that may help us then let's blow the place to pieces." Hockface says.

"Before you mention anything Jacob, this is not gonna be like last time, we actually set off the explosives after we leave." She continues.

"Good." He responds.

"I'll stick outside here keeping a lookout for any guards that approach, would anyone like to join?" Hockface asks.

Three rebels do so Hockface signals them to join her as the other rebels walk in, now there are two rebels standing on the sides of the entrance to the base.

Inside the base, things look dilapidated and run down with the walls feeling like concrete and looking a vanilla colour, despite that though, in the main lobby area of the base, there's a bunch of holographic maps each showing the places of rebel bases across Edalbire with a note on a table reading 'Take these back ASAP!'

Ignoring that, the rebels continue down and come across a bunch of rooms all with different labels on them:

'Interrogation room 1'

'Interrogation room 2'

'Table room'

'Secret room'
"Ok, there's eight of us so we each go in pairs into each room? That sound good with everyone." A rebel says.
All of them nod.
Jacob and one rebel go into 'Interrogation room 1' and the others go into pairs into the other rooms.

Once inside the room, it doesn't look like a typical interrogation room, instead there's just a chair and the door, however under the chair is a note, Jacob notices it, picks it up and reads it.
"To the soldier who is in charge of the interrogations, you have been given permission to go even further with them, do whatever you want to get prisoners to confess to their crimes....in short....do whatever the hell you want and get as creative as you want with your interrogations.
"God damn, they were probably some sick bastards." The rebel with Jacob responds.
"Yeah, they were." Jacob replies with sorrow in his voice, was he one of the soldiers who did that? If so then it's very clear that by the tone of his voice that he regrets it.
"Hey, you ok?" The rebel asks Jacob.
"Y..y...yeah, I am...what's your name by the way?" Jacob asks.
"You'll probably recognise mine....Connor" He says.
"That name sounds familiar but...why does it?" Jacob responds.
"You may know my sister...Gasmask...?" Connor replies.
"Wait a second....YOU'RE her younger brother?" Jacob responds with major surprise in his voice.
Instead of saying anything, Connor nods.
"Fuck....just know that....i'm very fucking sorry about what I did."
Jacob says with major regret and sorrow in his voice.
"Jacob...as much as I hate what you did...I know that you had no choice, I don't hold it against you." Connor responds.

"...Thank you." Jacob says.

After taking a deep breath they both continue looking but can't find anything else, however they do take the note with them once they leave the room.

When they're back in the lobby, they're greeted by an empty space, however the alarm is still going off and soldiers can be heard coming from both sides of the room so the two get out their guns and start getting ready to fire, at which point as soon as they see the soldiers coming, they start firing and from the two rebels plus all the guards, gunshots are being thrown left and right and all over the place. Jacob and Connor are able to hold them off for a bit but soon they start closing in.

"Shit, we need to do something, quick." Jacob says in a panic.

"I've got an idea and I need you to trust me on this." Connor responds.

"There's no other choice right now, Connor." Jacob responds.

After that, Connor jumps on Jacob then does a frontflip behind the guards coming from the direction that Jacob is facing, while also taking out a bunch in the air with Jacob helping take out soldiers that are running in the direction that Connor is flying in.

A few minutes after the soldiers were taken out, the other rebels came out of the rooms that they were in.

"Can't check what we have now, there may be more on the way." Jacob says

After saying that, the rebels start running out of the base and placing explosives on the walls as they're running out and when they get out, Hockface and the three other rebels that were standing guard run with the ones who came out, once they're back at the car, Callum activates the explosives and watches as the base goes down.

"Woooo, that's our part of the mission completed, now let's head back to the base, we can show each other what we found there." Hockface says as she and the other rebels get in the car.

In a different part of the country, Gothboy is standing by with their team.
"Right, we just got the go ahead that the breaking in team has finished, time for us to start our side of it and once we're done, we let the assassination team now, by then they should be done with their scout out." Gothboy says.
After saying that, Gothboy signals for the rebels to move forward as they do, they ready their guns and rather than sneak around the wall like the breaking in team did, they just find the entrance to the base and kick it open.

"Congratulations, you've won a contest for a free holiday." Gothboy says.
"Oh? To where?" A guard says.
"DESTINATION FUCKED!!!!" They say as the rebels just start opening fire on the guards, at which point the alarm goes off and the team split off into three groups covering all parts of the base.
After each part has been confirmed to be clear, some rebels stay out while the others rush in and kick in the doors to each room.
"Two choices: Come back with us for questioning or die." Each rebel says as they see soldiers unarmed, some refuse to go and spit or insult the rebels so they get shot, however others do go with them.
Once everything had been confirmed to be cleared, the rebels who went in start to come out, however they are soon after bombarded by soldiers right before they could get to the exit.

"You really thought you could do this and live?" One soldier asks in a cocky tone.

"Well actually, yeah." A rebel responds.

"Ohhhh, well that's too bad because this is your final resting place." The soldier says as each one pulls their guns out and the rebels go into cover, as soon as they're ready, they start firing.

"Shit, we need a plan and quick." Riley says as the rebels briefly go up and shoot the soldiers that are shooting at them, some rebels get damaged, a few are even killed in the line of fire, the same however also applies for the soldiers.

"Wait, I've just had an idea." Riley says.

"Go on." Gothboy continues while everyone is shooting.

"If this base is like the other one then around the back, there should be a little weak point, all we'd need is an explosive to exploit it or someone incredibly strong." They continue saying in a panic.

"Did you just say explosive?" Gothboy asks.

"Yeah, why, do you have one?" Riley responds.

"I always carry one on me." Gothboy says.

"Sweet, all we need is some way to get to the other side of the base." Riley responds.

"Ok then, we need some way to distract the soldiers." Gothboy repeats.

"COME ON GUYS, THINK OF SOMETHING, WE CAN'T HOLD THEM OFF MUCH LONGER!!!" A rebel shouts from the other end of the cover.

In the chaos, a rebel throws a smoke grenade which causes the rebels enough time to make it to the back of the base without getting seen, at which point they set off the explosives, hide around the side with another smoke grenade getting thrown then set off, once the smoke from the explosion has cleared, the rebels make their way to the back of the base and get out, once the rebels are out, they make their way back to the car.

"Right, stick those soldiers in the back, we need to interrogate them back at the base." Gothboy says as some rebels get in the car while others stay at the base.

"Hey, why are some of you staying here?" Gothboy asks.

"We're gonna need a few to hold down the fort and get rid of the bodies that piled up during our fight so it may as well be us, plus we could all take it in turns once everything is ready." A rebel says.

"Very well, we'll see you all later then." Gothboy says, once they said that, the car drives off with the two rebels waving.

"Right, time to let the assassination team know." One rebel says.

Another rebel gets their walkie talkie out.

"Team three: Your turn asssation team." The rebel says.

"Got it, thanks for letting us know." Gasmask says into her walkie talkie.

"We've had plenty of time to figure this out and we're going with plan A right?" Gasmask says.

The other three rebels there who are a part of team three nod in agreement.

After agreeing, all three sneak into an abandoned and practically destroyed looking city and follow the figures but hiding in the process.

"Why would some high profile figures for the king even meet in a place like this." A rebel whispers.

"My guess is to avoid raising suspicions in a highly populated area cause well...i'm pretty sure you've seen how ruggedly everyone usually dresses, those lot would clearly stand out if they met in a place like Segiru which is a highly populated area." Gasmask replies.

"I'll give you that one." The rebel replies.

After a few minutes the figures all go into a building, Gasmask pulls out a grappling hook, grapples to the top of the building then throws it down to the other rebels, all of which do the same and when the final one is up on the roof, they give it back to Gasmask.

The roof is completely flat except for a ventilation system which isn't active at that point.

After noticing it, one of the rebels goes to a secret panel on the back of the vent, enters a few things and the vents start.

"What are you doing?" Gasmask asks.

"Making the plan easier, I'm assuming that we have the knockout grenades?" That rebel responds.

"Yeah, why do.......OHHHHHHHHHHHHHHHHHHHHHHHH." Gasmask realises the plan.

After she realises, she hands one of the knockout grenades to the rebel who throws it inside the vent, at which point they go back to the behind of it and shut it off.

"How did you do that?" A different rebel asks.

"Easy: Right before everything went to absolute shit, I used to work here....ok, slight lie, this was actually a family business that went bust after the King publicly executed my parents." That rebel says with a hint of sadness in their voice.

"Hey, hey, it's ok, once the king has been overthrown, you can rebuild and start the place up anew and make it better then it was before, i'm sure that your parents would love that and who knows...maybe you'll even have a kid to hand it down to when you get older. That rebel says, pulling the other one into a hug.

"Thank you." The two are now hugging.

"Er, guys, as much as I love wholesome stuff, we kinda have A mission right now." Gasmask reminds them.

"Oh right." They part from the hug and each rebel starts making their way inside the building via the ventilation system.

Once inside, they're greeted with the remnants of what used to be a cosy and friendly cafe, however due to what happened, the table has now been nearly destroyed, the pictures on the walls are ruined and the bright yellow on the walls has now faded into a much darker shade.

Once each rebel as the unconscious bodies on the floor, they all kill them, either via twisting their neck, shooting a pistol with a silencer on them or by slicing their necks open.

Once every target has been taken care of, the rebel whose family ran the business takes a proper look around.

"Fuck, I missed this place...Alot of my childhood memories are here and now look what bastard excuse of a king has done!" The rebel says.

"Hey, your friend's right, when the king has been overthrown, you can come back here and rebuild it." Gasmask says in an attempt to comfort the rebel.

"Oh by the way, what's your name?" She asks.

"...Blaine." They respond.

"Blaine Chiuku." They continue.

"So your family was the one who owned this place?" Gasmask asks.

"Yep, I was supposed to inherit it after my parents passed away and well...I sorta did but...that didn't last too long because A: Grieving and B: Well...the king kinda ordered a nuclear test on this small town, I was lucky to make it out alive and so were a few others, however most people weren't so lucky." They say, clearly trying not to cry.

"If you look all around in the other buildings, you'll see the skeletons of people who that wanker killed, innocent fucking lives he took, without a second though, a whole fucking town, gone in an instant." They say, trying really hard not to shout.

"Blaine, once we've accomplished our goal, you can come back here and rebuild the cafe and hell who knows, it may even prompt people to come here and help rebuild this town to what it once was." Gasmask says.

"You...sure?" Asks Blaine timidly.

"Yeah, you know what, when we're done, I'll even help with it, how does that sound?" She continues.

"R...r...really? Are you sure about that?" Blaine asks Gasmask.

"Oh yeah, we'll all help." The rest of the rebels say in agreement.

Instead of saying anything, Blaine bursts into tears and hugs them.

Ten minutes later, they stop crying, take a deep breath and swallow.

"Thank you guys." They say, in a very clearly happy tone.

"You're welcome." Gasmask responds.

"Now, we should probably get out of here and meet the others back at the base." She continues.

Each rebel nods in agreement and as such, they take the same way out that they did to get in.

Although Blaine takes a quick look around the place before going back up.

"I'll be back soon." They say to themself before grappling themself up.

Once all three teams are back at the base, Gothboy sends the soldiers that their team caught downstairs into an interrogation room.

"I'll be heading down in a minute, I'm just a bit peckish." Gothboy says as she grabs something to eat and eats it down on the way to the interrogation room.

Once there, she is greeted by all the soldiers that her team brought in sat on one end of an empty table and she sits on the other end.

"Well, well, well, I honestly never thought we'd have a use for this room but damn, I was wrong." Gothboy exclaims.

"Whatever it is you want, we're not gonna say." A soldier says.

"Oh, is that so? Well then, I'll just be on my way." Gothboy gets up as they say that and walks to the door but instead of opening it to leave, they lock it.

"Oops, silly me, I locked it, guess we're gonna have to wait." They say as they sit down.

"So, what would you like to talk about?" They ask.

"Bite me." A second soldier with a slightly deeper voice says.

"No thanks, I'm not a cannibal, if you can't think of anything then I have plenty of conversation topics for you." They say.

"First thing on my list: Aside from the king, is there anyone else you work for?" They ask.

No response from any of them.

"Now, i'm no expert in stuff like this but if my experience from before everything went to shit has taught me anything, it's that when someone is silent on a question like that, they're usually hiding something so I'll ask again and this time I want an answer." They say, starting to get slightly agitated.

Still no response.

"Well, I did give you an easy choice and if you had taken it, all of us probably would have been out by now but nope, you had to select the hard way so don't complain to me." Gothboy says

After saying that, Gothboy gets their pistol out from their pocket, slides the top bit and then shoots at the wall.

"You really don't think I'd shoot you? I already did with some of your friends, don't think i'd make any exceptions for you lot." She says with slight anger in her voice.

"Try it." The guard in the middle says as they also pull their gun out and once they both have their pistols out, they are aiming them at each other's heads.

"Mate, she's unhinged, it's probably best not to provoke her." A different soldier says.

"Ugh, what do you know?" The soldier with their pistol out says as they shoot that one's hand.

"He deserves it." The soldier that shot says.

"You bastard!" Both that soldier and Gothboy says, however it's easy to tell that, that soldier is nearly in tears.

No response from either end.

"I'll give you one more chance." Gothboy says.

"Say what you know, if you don't then I won't hesitate to shoot you." Gothboy says.

It's clear in the soldier's eyes that they are trying really hard not to break.

"I'd much rather die than tell you what I know." That soldier says.

"Very well then, don't say I didn't give you any chances." Gothboy then shoots that soldier in the end and they fly back to the ground, dead.

Each soldier then has a panicked look in their eyes.

"Heh, judging by your eyes, I'm guessing that you don't want that fate,before I ask that question again, I have another one for you all." Gothboy says.

"Do any of you actually want to be soldiers?" They ask with a calm voice.

Although reluctantly, each soldier shakes their head, indicating to Gothboy that they didn't want to be soldiers for the king.

"So, how about I cut you lot a deal, if you tell me what I want to know then i'll help you get out of the country and get to the next one over where you can forget about your lives here and start anew over there, don't worry, we have contacts there to set it up so we'll be able to do it easily." Gothboy continues.

"There is also another option, you could also join us in the rebellion, your choices." They finish.

After a few minutes of huddled whispers, each soldier agrees to leave the country and start anew.

"Very well but before I can let you do that, can you tell me what I want to know?" Gothboy says.

"Yeah, there were a few, most of us were really hired/freelance killers before we joined the king's soldiers, however we often killed our targets should they not give their money, the king wouldn't have been any exception." A soldier says.

"I doubt there would be many that you'd be interested in...although, there is one and that was the one who even got us in contact with the king, he may be of use to you, None of us know his name, however we do have a picture of him." At that point, one of the soldiers passes a picture of a well dressed man in a monochrome suit with very smart hair.

"What was his goal with you?" Gothboy asks.

"He commissioned us to gather intel on the rebels then pass it over, if i'm to guess though, i'd say that he was to give said intel to the king and what he'd use it for, we have no idea." The same soldier asks.

"Thanks for answering, I did have a few follow ups but you already answered them with the freelancer/hired killer thing." Gothboy says.

After saying that, she gets up and unlocks the door.

"Wait here, soon someone will be by to pick you up and take you to a secret boat we have that flies under the radar, at which point, they'll take you to Tectlauv, once there, you'll be given everything you need to start new lives." Gothboy says.

Meanwhile, in Science Lab's lab, he's working on a project, something most likely intended for the rebels, however whatever it is, he's keeping it a secret from the other people in the lab with him, suddenly and out of no-where, a shadowy figure starts speaking to him.

"Science lab? Am I mistaken?" It says, it's voice is somewhat deep, however it's very easy to tell that whoever it is, they have a voice modifier which is masking their usual voice, whoever it is clearly knows him and knows that he'll recognise their voice should they use their normal voice.

"Yeah? Who's this and how do you know who I am?" He asks in a concerned voice.

"That is not important right now, what is important though is how you're being treated, didn't you say to yourself the other day that they'll just abandon you?" The voice says.

Upon hearing that, Science lab goes back in surprise and falls onto the floor, landing on his ass.

"What the- how did you hear that? I was just venting to myself." He says in surprise.

The figure brings it's arm out of the shadow's on their hand is a giant scar, Science lab gets back up without holding onto the hand.

"I didn't need any help, plus why are you even here?" He asks, starting to get annoyed.

"Oh my mistake, I am here to make you an offer, one that you.....*can't* refuse." It says in a mysterious tone.

"What...do you mean?" Science lab asks.

"I mean this." A gun comes out from the shadows and fires but instead of a bullet being shot, a tranquilliser is shot into his neck from the shadows, after he's knocked unconscious, Proto gets annoyed and attempts to paralyse the figure but is unable to and gets kicked from the shadow to the wall by the entrance and is knocked out as a result. At that point, the figure grabs Science lab by the legs and drags him away.

A few hours later, rebels are just hanging out and chatting in the base, others are out on solo missions, including Gothboy, however soon an alarm goes off but, it's not a normal mission alarm, instead a different alarm goes off, a more intense and sounding one and an announcement on a PA system.

"EVERYONE TO THE MISSION BRIEFING ROOM, NOW! THIS IS NOT A DRILL, REPEAT, THIS IS NOT A DRILL! EVERYONE TO THE MISSION BRIEFING ROOM, NOW!!!!"

Not too long later, everyone is in the mission briefing room and Vetry is trying really hard not to cry with Alfie giving them comfort, amongst all of that, each rebel is talking over each other and no-one can hear anything.

"QUIETTTTT!!!!!!" Hockface shouts and after that, everyone shuts up.

"I'm sorry, also I get that you're all confused about what's happened and I plan to explain in just a few minutes, I just need to confirm two things first." She responds and then leaves the room.

Outside in the hallway, she's on the phone.

"Are you one hundred percent sure that's what's happened?" She asks someone.

"Fuck, everyone's confused and who knows how they're gonna react when they find out." Hockface says in a panic.

"And you're absolutely sure that those two aren't involved at all?" Hockface also asks.

"Right....very well then, I'll let the rebels know then." She says.

After that, she puts the phone down, stands in the middle of the room and swallows.

"I didn't want to do this but...I have some very crap news that I know none of you want to hear." She says.

At that point, she brings up a picture of Science Lab.

"Our amazing scientist and inventor: Science lab....has been kidnapped..." She says with her voice shaking.

After hearing that, the rebels suddenly start all talking over each other again in chaos and confusion.

Chapter 4: Receive and Turn You Part 1

"JACOB! ALFIE! RILEY! REPORT TO YOUR ROOMS NOW!!!" A voice over a loudspeaker can be heard, the voice sounds feminine and very dominant, however there is a hint of innocence towards it but that can only be heard by those who are actually trying to hear it.

After the three don't return, the voice shouts that out again and it keeps looping in the same tone for five minutes until the alarms in the castle go off, all the guards leave their rooms and stand outside of their rooms in an attention pose, as if they were in some sort of army getting ready to defend their country.

While most of the soldiers are standing outside their rooms in what would usually be a giant, empty hallway, there are three doors which has no-one standing there.

Upon hearing the alarm, the king goes to the doors.

"YOU THREE, GET OUT HERE, NOW!!!" Despite him shouting that in a very pissed off tone, there was no response coming from the rooms.

"YOU THREE, OPEN THE DOOR NOW!" He shouts at three of the guards who are standing next to him and without hesitation, all three of them do open the doors but when they're open, they find that the rooms have been vacated, almost as if they're a hotel room and that would be because the Alfie, Jacob and Riley aren't actually in the castle anymore.

"What the fuck?" The king says in a calm but still very pissed off tone.

"It would seem that the three soldiers who stayed in this room are no longer here!" One soldier says in a calm but very scared tone with a slight hint of masculinity towards his voice.

"Oh, I thought that they were definitely in there, do forgive me for my stupidity." The king replies in a very sarcastic tone.

"You are forgive-" The guard starts to say but is then cut off by The King.
"I was being sarcastic, you dumbass." He replies.
"Anyway, search EVERY ROOM, NO-ONE goes to sleep until we find those three!" He shouts as he walks out of the room, slamming the double doors at the end of the hallway behind him.
In a panic, everyone starts splitting up and going to different rooms of the castle.

The next morning, soldiers are still searching, however they haven't had any luck finding three that have gone missing, however one soldier outside has noticed a hole in the moat of the castle.
"What the-" the soldier says to themself, after noticing the hole, as such, they begin to investigate and follow it, only to find that it leads to where the three got out, alongside that.
"So...I wonder if this is how they got out? Sneaky bastards, how long were they digging this and how did they get away with it?" The soldier says to themself, after which, they go back the way they went in the pull out a walkie-talkie.
"Everyone, you're gonna want to see this, I think I found out what happened to the three." The soldier says.
Soon after, everyone is by the moat.
"Let me just get right to the point, the three went through the hole down here and came out the other end which leads to the rest of the country." The soldier says.
"And you know how?" The King asks.
"I went through the hole myself then placed two and two together after seeing what was on the other side." The soldier replies.
"I see, I had a feeling that something like this would happen sooner or later." The king says.
"What do you mean Your Highness?" The soldier asks.

"None of your business, anyway, fill this hole up so no-one leaves without permission again." The king responds.
"Very well." The soldier responds and starts to fill up the hole, not asking anymore questions.

A few days later, in the king's room, an alarm goes off and on some CCTV footage that comes out of the roof, rebels can be seen breaking into bases that are holding some top secret information that if got out, could be catastrophic to his reign and as such, the presses a button on the wall, which sounds an alarm and brings down a speaker mic.
"EVERYONE GEAR UP AND GET OUT THERE, FIND THE REBELS AND KILL THEM!!!!! AND IF YOU FIND JACOB, RILEY AND ALFIE, KILL THEM AS WELL!!!" The king shouts into the mic, after which rapid footsteps can be heard from outside of the room.
"If that's how you wanna play Blood Renegades then so be it, I can play dirty as well, just you watch." the king says to himself while looking out of the window and into the distance.

"And what about me sir?" A mysterious figure asks.
"Get this guy and bring him here, by any means necessary, I'll expect him back when I return." The king says as he places a picture into the hand of a shadowy figure, once said picture is in the hand, The King then leaves the room and heads to a destroyed looking city, he is looking around for a specific building and once he finds said building, he walks into a destroyed office and once in there, he takes a seat and goes into thought, as if he's waiting for someone or...multiple people.

A few hours later, two well dressed people walk in, they both are wearing black and white suits, although one has their hair done up like a ponytail while the other has it flat and going across their eyes, meanwhile the one with the ponytail has sunglasses on so it's impossible to see their eyes, almost as if they're trying to keep their identities a secret and as such, there's no revealing features on their faces, if there was any then whoever did their makeup extraordinarily well.

"Welcome, I do hope your trip here wasn't too eventful." The king says in a polite tone.

"It was not eventful." The person with their hair in their eyes says in a monotone voice.

"In that case, I trust the Blood Renegades didn't give you any problems?" The king asks in the same tone.

"No they did not." The person with the ponytail says in the same tone.

"That's good, anyway enough idle chatter, let's get down to business, I assume that you have the money?" The king says.

Instead of saying anything, the person with the ponytail pulls up a suitcase and opens it to reveal a bunch of notes with King Charles iii's face on it.

"Thank you and as promised, here's the documents." The king hands over an envelope marked 'PRIVATE'.

"I trust the envelope has the stuff in there to kill that magician?" The king asks.

The two people open the envelope and see the documents which have all they need.

"Yes." The person with the hair over their eyes says.

"Now I have one question for you two." The king says

"Of all people, why come to me, you could have gone to any assassin in the world." The king responds.

"Because I know how much of a personal hatred you have against him Your Highness and that you would not pass up an opportunity to kill him." The person with the ponytail says.

"I see, well in that case, hopefully this does kill him, have a safe trip back." The king responds.

After which, all three leave the building then go their separate ways, however while walking back, he notices two dead bodies in a diner.

"What the-" He walks into it and examines them, only to realise who they are.

"Oh fuck off." He exclaims.

After fully identifying them both, he storms out of the diner and runs back towards the castle.

Soon after, he arrives then runs back into his room and opens up a holographic computer, on it he looks up many of the bases he has and finds the rebels and his soldiers in a massive fight at one of them and instead of doing anything, he just watches as people on both sides get killed and the rebels eventually making it out of there using a smoke grenade.

"Run run as fast as you can rebels, you may be able to win the battle but you have yet to win the war." The king says to himself.

A few hours later, a voice comes from a shadow.

"Here is the item you requested, Your Highness, now I trust you have my payment as always?" The figure says.

Without saying a word The King hands the money to a shadowy figure and once said figure has it, Science Lab is pushed out of the shadows.

"Ah am I in the presence of the esteemed Science Lab, greatest inventor and scientist in all of Edalbire?" The king asks sarcastically, knowing full well who's standing in front of him.

"Bite me." Science lab says in response.

"Oh come on now, that's no way to speak to someone." The king responds.

"I don't care." Science Lab says in response to that.

"I should have expected that, anyway, I suppose you're wondering why I called you here." The king says.

"I have a few guesses but go on." Science lab responds.

"It's simple, you're gonna put your intelligence and expertise to good use for your country." The king then responds in a slightly menacing tone.

"And what if I refuse?" Science lab asks curiously.

"Oh, you can't." The king then says in response.

"I...can't? Just what do you mean?" He asks.

"Oh it's just as it sounds on the tin, if you refuse to do what I ask then you will go back to the rebels but not like this, oh no, you'll be going back in a body bag." The King then says.

Hearing that, Science Lab goes back in shock.

"What the fuck!??!" Science lab says in a very surprised tone.

"Why did you even bring me here in the first place?" He asks.

"Well, two reasons actually; A: Leverage against the rebels/Blood Renegades and B: Because didn't you say yourself that you feel like you'll just be abandoned?" The king responds.

"What the- How did you-" Science Lab says in the same tone as before.

"Oh it's easy, because the OS for your little robot friend isn't finished yet, I hacked into it and it's now basically a camera for me and no-one knows, not even the robot itself." The king says.

"You son of a-" Science lab has a face that looks like he's ready to attack the king but two soldiers stand in his way.

"Now now, let's not be hasty, when you're working under me, you don't have to worry about being abandoned ever again or anyone mistreating you, because you'll be creating stuff for our side, you'll be treated with the utmost respect from the soldiers." The king says.

"I'll be treated with....the utmost respect?" Science lab responds with a tone that says that he is considering taking the King's offer of joining.

"If I do, can you promise me one thing?" Science lab asks.

"Go on." The king responds.

He whispers something into the king's ear.

"If it's just that one thing then yes, I can guarantee it, I am a man of my word." The king says

"In that case then.....Yes, I will join you." Science Lab responds with his eyes closed and facing the floor.

"Wonderful, now let me take you to your new work station." The king says as he guides Science lab out of the room and down the corridor to a room at the end of it, once in it, he's greeted by a room that looks very similar to his old one but the walls are a very dark blue colour instead the metallic silver that his work room has in the Blood Renegades base and all the tables are laid out as if it was a classroom and not a laboratory.

"Anything you need, just let me know and it'll be provided." The king says as he leaves the room and at that point, Science Lab just looks around the room to get an idea of how to navigate the room and maybe even some secret escapes.

"Wait, Your Highness, one question quickly." Science lab says and just before the king is out of earshot, he turns around.

"Yeah?" He asks.

"What exactly do I need to work on?" Science lab.

"Oh fuck, I knew I forgot to tell you something." After saying that, The King returns to the lab and gives Science Lab a USB stick and a laptop.

"On this USB stick are blueprints for different weapons and vehicles for our soldiers oh and if you so chose, when they're ready and complete, you could even keep a few for yourself." The king responds.

"So, anything else?" He asks.

"Actually, one thing: Where do I sleep?" Science Lab asks.

"Just for tonight, in here, however tomorrow, you'll be getting your own private and smart bedroom all to yourself." He responds.

"Wait....seriously?!?!?" Science lab says in a very surprised tone.

"Yep, so any more questions?" The king asks.

"Nope, not right now." Science lab says.

"Very well, if you need me for anything, just press the blue button on your desk." The king says as he leaves the room and once he's left, Science Lab boots up the laptop, logs into the account assigned to him then puts in the USB stick to see the blueprints, when browsing he sees stuff relating to powerful guns, swords, tanks, helicopters, cars, boats and more.

"Holy shit, guess I'd better get started then, hmm...what to work on first...." Science lab says out loud to themself.

Meanwhile in another part of the castle the King is in his room and talking to a mysterious shadowy figure on a giant screen.

"I trust everything is in place?" The figure asks.

"Not exactly..." The king responds.

"What do you mean? For RD-2 to actually work, it needs a Sonic soundwave disrupter fixed and working." The figure responds in a frustrated tone.

"Well somehow, the old inventor managed to escape the castle, however don't worry, I have since found a new inventor and I plan to take precautions to make sure that escape doesn't happen again." The King responds.

"See that it doesn't, because you know what will happen if RD-2 fails don't you?" The figure asks in a very threatening tone.

"Indeed I do, don't worry though, I'll make sure that the Sonic soundwave disrupter is finished by the deadline."

"See that you do." The figure says, after which point the screen turns off and the king kicks a chair.

"FUUUUUUUUUCK!!!!!" He shouts extremely loudly while kicking a chair to the other side of the room and it slamming into a wall.

"If those three shits for brains didn't leave then we'd have it done by now." He shouts to a guard just standing there.

"YES SIR!" The guard shouts.

Suddenly, an idea comes to the king's mind.

"Guard, I have a special job for you." He says, with a very evil smirk on his face and an evil look in his eyes, it's clear that whatever he's planning, it's not gonna be good for the guard.

"Track down those three shits for brains and..." His tone changes to a very dark and evil tone, any messing around that he had been doing up until that point was now gone "...Execute them by any means necessary."

The guard had a clear look of fear in his eyes, he was scared and he had clearly seen this tone before; that being said however, not wanting to risk being killed himself, he left the room and did what the king asked him to do, not long after that, the king left the room.

Meanwhile, in the lab which Science lab was working in, he had managed to find the blueprints and had already started work on a prototype for one of the weapons, the weapon looks like a Tommy Gun, while in the process of printing the prototype, the king walks in the room.

"So, any progress?" The king asks, trying not to sound annoyed as he didn't want to let it out on Science Lab.

"Actually, yeah, alot because I am currently in the process of printing out a prototype for one of the weapons in the blueprints." Science Lab exclaims in an faux excited tone.

"Oh? Which one?" The king asks, genuinely intrigued.

"The TMDG" he responds.

"The Tommy Detonator Gun?" The King asks.

"Yeah but uhh...why is it called that?" Science lab asks, with both a confused look on his face and a confused tone in his voice.

"Cause it launches grenades." The king responds.

"Then shouldn't it be called the TMGGL; Tommy Gun Grenade Launcher?" Science lab says.

The look on the king's face first turns to one of slight anger at being talked back to but after he thought clearly, the face turns relieved. "Honestly, that's a really good point, feel free to change the name." There is no anger in his voice, only slight annoyance relating to the fact that he didn't think of it first and that it took a kidnapped scientist for the name to come up.

After he says that, the gun stops printing and Science lab loads the gun.

"You're gonna wanna stand behind me for this Your Highness" He says as he aims the gun at a target that's in the far end of the room, once fired the plasma grenade shoots out, hits the target and makes a large purply explosion that would have usually destroyed the room but thanks to the target being in a specially locked room, the explosion was only contained to that one room.

"So, what do you think?" Science Lab asks.

"I'll give you this: That was fucking amazing, how long do you think you'll be before the TMGGL is ready for mass production amongst the minions?" The king asks rather enthusiastically.

"I'm not sure really cause as mentioned before, this is only the prototype, I do have to work out a bunch of kinks with it to get it perfected, not only that but the design itself would also need changing cause while yeah, a tommy gun is a good design, this specific model can only hold up to two grenades max and i'm pretty sure you're minions are gonna want more than that." He replies.

"So TL;DR...I don't know how long it'll take before it's ready for mass production and I don't like guessing, I want to be 100% certain." He says.

"Gotcha." And with that, the king walks out of the room, slightly annoyed but still understanding.

Meanwhile, a hooded figure walks out of one of the shadows in the new science lab.

"Greetings Science lab, I am so glad that I finally have the honour of meeting you...again" The figure says in a mysterious tone

"What the- Who are you?" He asks in a very shocked tone, the look of surprise on Science Lab's face as well goes to show that despite this person apparently knowing him from somewhere before.

"I'm surprised you don't know...anyway, that's not important right now, what is important is that I make your stay here as comfortable as possible." The figure says in the same mysterious and suspicious tone.

"Let me guess, you're under the order of The King to do this?" Science Lab asks.

"Not...necessarily." The figure says, tone not changing.

"I see and what exactly do you mean by 'Comfortable'?" He asks with a confused look on his face and a concerned tone in his voice.

"Simple; just giving you what you want when you need it and allowing you to do what you want to do." The figure says, still in a mysterious and suspicious tone.

"Ok then, there's just one thing right now." Science lab says with a slightly confident tone in his voice and his fists as well as a cocky look on his face.

"And that is?" The figure asks.

"How do you know me?" Science lab asks in a slightly cocky tone.

"I'm afraid....I can't answer that." The tone of the figure's voice changes, almost as if...they wanted to say it but something is stopping them, what is stopping them however is unknown.

"Are you okay?" Science lab ask, this time he has both a concerned tone in his voice and a concerned look on his face.

"Yeah I am, you should not have to worry about me, it's not your job for I am just merely a lowly bounty hunter who goes from gig to gig." The figure says back in the same mysterious and suspicious tone as before.

"If you're sure then that's fine, however if you want to vent then I won't mind." Science lab says as he goes back to work on a weapon he's building for The King.

"....Thank you...you're just as nice as I remember..." The figure says the second part under their breath so Science lab is unable to hear it, despite that however, he does know that they did say something.

"You're welcome, although did you say something?" He asks in a concerned voice.

"....No." The figure replies, clearly lying.

Science lab latches onto the fact that the figure is lying but decides not to do anything about it, mostly because the figure most likely does not want to talk about it and trying to force someone to talk about something when they don't want to...Yeah, Science Lab knows first hand just how mentally damaging that can be to someone and just how much it can ruin the trust between the people involved, especially between the one being forced to talk against their will...

In a school playground, there's a young Science lab, instead of being in his science gear, he's instead wearing a bowtie with a white shirt on under it, a blazer which has a school crest on it as well as some smart shoes and black trousers, not only that but his hair is also blonde instead of strawberry red, he doesn't have a gasmask on him at all so his entire face is visible now and he has an innocent smile on his face as well as brown eyes, despite the innocent smile however, he does have a very worried look on his face.

"Oi, freckleface" A voice is coming from behind Science Lab, it sounds like someone is attempting to do a very bad 1950s brooklyn greaser accent, upon hearing that accent, he immediately turns around and notices someone in a similar uniform to his but their clothes aren't as tidy as his is as their clothes are all messed up and the blazer is only on arm, there's also no bowtie on them which is a part of the school dress code and this person has light brown eyes, a lollipop stick hanging from their mouth, two earrings, light green hair and a pissed off look on their face.

"Watcha think you're doing huh?" The person says as they get closer to him.

"Uhh...uhhh....uhhh..." Science lab can't respond at all, almost as if he's scared of this person.

"Answer me huh? Or are you fucking deaf?" The person hits science Lab in the face and he falls down onto the ground with tears forming.

"W...w...what did I d...d...do?" Science Lab asks.

"Easy; you didn't answer when I asked you a simple fuckin question."
Still pissed off

After Science lab doesn't respond, he is punched again.

"I'm s...s...s...sorry C...c...c...cyrus." Science lab says while trying not to cry.

"Henry, Henry, Henry...you need to learn to speak when your betters are addressing you, you're just lucky you ain't in that castle up there"
Cyrus points to a castle.

"I hear that they do much worse to people like you up there." He says.

"L...l...like what?" Henry asks in a very worried tone, almost as if they're trying really hard not to cry.

"Worse than me; by that I mean torture..." Cyrus says.

"N...n...no, it's not true, the royal family are n...n...nice." Henry says.

"That's just what they seem like when on the TV but answer me this: Have you even seen them behind closed doors?" Cyrus asks in a very condescending tone and right up in Henry's face.

"N...n...no." Henry responds.

"Exactly." Cyrus says in the same condescending tone

"And their daughter? Oh, trust me buddy; She's the worst out of all of them, she may have the look of your typical princess but in reality, she's a massive bitch and so damn evil." Cyrus continues.

"Now, now Henry..." He bends down to his level and looks Henry in the eyes

"I know that you don't want to talk about the shit that's bothering you, however as your *'friend'* I don't care about that, you will talk about the shit, otherwise my two friends here.." Cyrus gets his fists ready to punch.

"....Would like to say hello again, and you know just how much they love you Henry." He says in a cocky tone.

After that he speaks in a high pitched tone. "Oh we just *love* you Henry and we love saying hello to you"

Instead of saying anything, Henry remains silent, it's clear that he doesn't want to talk about the stuff that's bothering him, despite that however Cyrus doesn't care and proceeds to punch Henry until his nose is bleeding and tears are streaming down his face.

"Now, will you tell me or do I have to get these ladies out again?" Cyrus says in the same condescending tone but also sounding pissed off at the same.

"N...n...n...no" Henry says, tears on his face, he's now crying like crazy.

"No, what freckleface?" Same tone as before, except Cyrus is now looking more pissed than before.

However, right before Cyrus can punch Henry again, someone grabs his fist.

"Why don't you pick on someone who's actually physically tougher than you, you coward, or are you just all bark and no bite?" This person had a very pissed off look on their face, their hair was red and very messy, their eyes are light green, they also have circle glasses on and instead of the school uniform however, they had a jean jacket on with a grey shirt underneath and a chain, on their bottom half, they have pitch black boots on as well as a skirt with tights covering their legs.

"Shit...Max...we were...uhhh..." Cyrus's tone suddenly changes from a cocky one to a scared one, it's clear that whoever this Max person is definitely scared Cyrus.

"Well, i'm listening." Max said, starting to get pissed off with Cyrus. Instead of responding, Cyrus just runs away screaming. "Knew it." Max looks down to Henry then bends to his level.

"Hey Henry, it's ok now, he's gone, i'm here to protect you." Max says as they plant a kiss on Henry's forehead and then sit down next to him, once sat down, Max pulls Henry into a side hug and Henry starts crying again, and in response, Max just strokes Henry's head.

"It's ok Henry, just let the tears out, it's perfectly ok to cry." Max said in a very calm tone.

After hearing that, Henry just starts crying uncontrollably. Instead of saying anything, Max just keeps on hugging Henry.

Back in the present day, Henry is leaning over the currently in production weapon that's laid out on the workbench and is trying really hard not to cry, the hooded figure however...is back in the shadows of the room and can't be seen.

"It's ok to cry Henry, you're perfectly valid when wanting to cry." That voice seemed to be in Henry's head and upon hearing it, he starts to cry again.

Chapter 5: Unwavering Belief

The briefing room; usually a peaceful place filled with rebels that's getting their next mission, not this time however...this time, it's filled with people going batshit insane over the news that Hockface just gave them..."Science lab was kidnapped? Surely it had to be some sort of joke right? Are we being bulshitted right now?" All those and more were some of the things each rebel was saying in-between all of the commotion.

"Everyone quiet" Hockface says with her voice raised, although slightly muffled due to the hockey mask, however no-one was able to hear her so she lifts the mask up slightly, to the point where her mouth is no longer covering it and repeats that with her voice more clearer.

Once she says that with a clearer voice, the room goes quiet and everyone focuses on Hockface.

"Thank you." She says as she breathes a sigh of relief. "Like I said, Science Lab has been kidnapped and now we have no leads on who did it and I know some of you are more than likely already getting ready to accuse the three new recruits, however there is no evidence pointing towards them and I don't want anyone planting any because of their past." She says in a stern voice.

"But it's obvious that they did it!" One of the rebels shouts, it's impossible to tell what they look like because of the dirt bike helmet and dark tint over their face, however clothes wise, they are wearing the usual equipment the rebels wear when they go out on missions.

"NO!" Hockface shouts. "That's exactly what I mean, blindly accusing without evidence isn't going to help anyone at all and for all we know, it could be someone very different; those three might not even be involved at all." She responds.

"Wait, Hockface, are you saying what I think you're saying?" Megan responds in surprise as she walks into the room.

"Yep, that's right...i'm saying that there may be a traitor among us....I swear, if someone makes that very fucking obvious joke..." Hockface replies in a stern tone and with a straight face, it's clear that she's being serious about the possibility of there being a traitor.

"Hehe, sus" A random rebel says quietly so that only those right next to them can hear and upon hearing their friend say that, the few rebels who could hear it laugh quietly.

After which, everyone the entire room starts speaking loudly again and everyone is talking all over each other.

"QUIET!!!" Hockface shouts again and as such, the entire room shuts up.

"Thank you" She says in relief, now as I was saying yes there is a traitor in our midst, however we have no idea who it is so don't go around swinging wild accusations, once there's enough evidence and we know who it is, i'll deal with them accordingly, the last thing we want is for this to get out because if it does then we can A: Say goodbye to the Blood Renegades and B: Say goodbye to our ultimate goal of putting the rightful queen on the throne" Hockface says in a stern voice. "Do I make myself clear?" She asks, in a starting to get annoyed type voice.

"YES MA'AM" every rebel in the room shouts as loud as they can.

"Good, right now we need to get ready for the next operation: Breaking Science lab out of the King's castle and bringing him back here so we can get ready for the final raid on the castle." Hockface mentions in an annoyed tone.

"So because of that, we need to split all of you up into teams again." She continues in the same tone.

"So, those of you who are good at full frontal attacks, please go to the right of the room, those who are best at strategizing please go to the centre and those who are best at sneaking and being stealthy please go to the left of the room, you'll each have your own team leaders who'll explain your missions, so I am gonna be the leader for the full frontal team, Gasmask will be the leader for the stealth team and Vetry here will be the leader for the strategizing team."

Each rebel goes to the different ends of the room that Hockface mentioned, a large chunk of the rebels are on the right side of the room while the middle and left parts of the room don't have as many rebels, however the left side does have many, meanwhile the centre only has six rebels.

"So if the other two teams could follow their leaders and my team follow me then we'll explain your missions and what you have to do." Hockface says.

As soon as she finishes saying that, the other two teams walk out of the room.

In the strategy room, Vetry is standing next to the mission assignment machine from before as well as the rebels that joined being spread round it.

"So, I don't need to explain what this machine does right?" Asked Vetry.

"Nope." Each rebel said in unison, unlike the other rebels who were going out into the field, these ones were just in their casual clothes, most likely because they don't need to wear any extra gear once in that room.

One of the rebels standing around the machine has light pink flat hair, a pumpkin hairclip, meanwhile their eyes are read and they have a curious look to them, their skin is pale like a vampire, meanwhile they have a dark green crop top on with the straps of their bra showing on their shoulders and they also have dark blue jeans as well as white, purple, black and yellow socks on and red and white trainers/sneakers.

"So our job is to basically help the frontline team with their roles from in here?" The pink haired rebel said.

"Sorta." Vetry replies.

"What we actually do is-..."

Before Vetry can finish talking, a dark blue screen pops up on all the TV's that were monitoring the security cameras which says: "**STAY TUNED FOR AN IMPORTANT ANNOUNCEMENT FROM HIS ROYAL HIGHNESS. DON'T TRY TO CHANGE THE CHANNEL, THIS IS PLAYING ON ALL FREQEUENCIES.**"

Upon reading that, Vetry tries to change the channels on each TV and lo and behold the message is still there and as such, they try the TV upstairs in the lounge and yep; it's also on there, same with the TV's others homes, it's now clear to Vetry that he ain't messing around with this broadcast.

Upon realising that, Vetry goes back down to the strategy room and waits around for the broadcast to start.

After a few minutes, a sound plays from the TV "**Greetings my royal subjects.**" There was no mistaking it, that was definitely the King's voice and usually when he did broadcasts like this...they were not good at all.

"**Now, as you all know, I like to think of myself as a fair and kind ruler and that i'm also lenient with certain things...**" Vetry scoffs after hearing that.

"**Well, it has come to my attention that the rebels known as the Blood Renegades like to abuse this kindness I offered so therefor, I am setting a curfew, affective immediately.**" The entire room gasps audible and Vetry gets ready to phone the frontline team.

"**Starting from 8PM and going until 9AM every day, there will be a curfew until EVERY SINGLE rebel is dead, my guards and the police have also been given permission to arrest anyone out of their homes after 8PM and before 9AM, not only that but if you resist, they have also been given the green light to execute on site.**" The entire room gasps again.

"Damnit..." One rebel says.

Vetry sighs. "Guys, I know that this may be bleak but it'll make our ultimate goal feel that much more sweeter when we eventually are able to succeed with it." They say, trying to encourage the rebels.

However the atmosphere in the room is mixed and instead of trying to force them to accept what they said, Vetry just gives a warm smile to each of them then continues watching."

"And furthermore, any rebel seen at all, no matter if it's outside of those curfew's or not, both the guards and the police have been given permission to execute on sight." The king continues.

"Should we warn the others?" One of the rebels says.

"No point, knowing hockface, she'll see it as some sorta challenge...same with alot of the other frontline rebels." Vetry replies, after which they sigh.

"I just hope they all come back safely." Vetry then says with a sad tone in their voice.

Upon realising the tone, the rebels that were already there sit Vetry down and try to comfort them...meanwhile...

"Oh, one more thing i'd like to share with you all today: We have captured many rebels already and not only that but we have also captured their families as well and each and every one of them should they be brought to the castle will all die a slow and painful death and no matter how much you plea, we will not stop until you all are dead." The king says menacingly.

"And not only that but we have the first person's family on the chopping block." Screams and cries can be heard in the distance.

"And the name of this lucky family is: Chester." After hearing that, the pink haired rebel is in absolute shock and has tears just streaming down their face.

"And I know you're still out there Quinn Chester so turn yourself in and I promise that I won't be as painful to you as I am to your family." The king says meancingly.

"**NO QUINN, DON'T, DON'T TURN YOURSELF IN!!!!**
HELP SAVE THE COUNTRY, SAVE EDALBIRE!!!!" One of the people screaming shouts after hearing the king

"**However due to the grotesque nature of this, we will not be showing it but just know that we WILL find you and when we do, you better hope it's the police and not one of my guards because if it's one of my guards then it's up to them what they do and I can't be held accountable for their actions.**" He says while the screams and cries can still be heard in the background and he's laughing evily.

"**Oh and one more thing, if anyone finds this girl and brings her to me...**" He shows a picture of A friendly looking young woman with a warm smile and ocean blue eyes in a regal dress along with very long and blonde hair, all tidy.

"**There is a chance that she has completely changed her identity and/or how she looks so keep that in mind, unfortunately I don't have any reference frame right now but as soon as I do then I will broadcast it for you all.**" The king says.

"**So with that, I bid you all adieu and remember, Viva La Edalbire!**" The broadcast shuts off after that sentence and everyone in the room is in absolute shock, especially Quinn who just started crying; upon realising that, everyone goes to comfort them.

But instead of saying stuff, they all just hug each other instead.

Around twenty minutes later, they get back up and sigh.

"Thanks guys..." Quinn says after crying

Regaining their composure, Quinn slaps their face and goes back to the mission assignment machine and speaks in a slightly confident tone "I don't think my family would want me moping about right now, not while he is still in power."

"You know Quinn, it's ok to not be ok." Vetry responds in a kind tone.

"I know but...I want to do this Vetry." Quinn responds, in a tone that is clearly conflicted, on one hand they do want to help the rebels out but on the other they don't and they just want to cry it out.

"Very well then." Everyone returns to the mission assignment machine and once there, Vetry proceeds to explain how the machine works to everyone.

"And right now, the frontline assault team are waiting for their objective, same with the stealth team, so out of these options, which would you all say is the best for our current situation."

Each option appears on the machine.

"DIRECT CASTLE SEIGE (NOT RECOMMENDED YET)"

"CASTLE SCOUTING (ONLY AVILABLE FOR THE STEALTH TEAM!)"

"DISTRACTION! (ONLY AVILABLE FOR THE FRONTLINE OFFENCE TEAM!)"

"GET THAT BLUE SUITED LAWYER WHO LIKES TO POINT AND CAN SUMMON WIND HERE AND TAKE THE KING TO COURT!!! (BOTH TEAMS!)"

"Oh, that's easy, the castle scouting for stealth and distraction for offense." One rebel says in a confident tone.

"Aw damn, I wanted to see that lawyer, rumour has it that he can even summon wind." Quinn responds in a faux disappointed tone.

"You mean like Airb-" A different rebel starts to say that.

"Aaaaaanyway, seeing as we've decided on the scouting and distraction, let's go and relay that information to the other teams, to do that we need to confirm our choices, after we've confirmed it, the other two teams will get the notifications on their ends via either their phones or their watches, depending which one they signed up." Vetry replies.

"I have a question though: What about Jacob and Riley?" Alfie says in a confused tone.

"What do you mean?" Vetry responds.

"Well, we only just joined the other day, would they have signed up already?" Alfie asks in the same tone.

"That i'm not sure about, you'd be better off asking them yourself when you get the opportunity later." Vetry responds in a calm and caring tone.

"Ah, no way to check it here?" Alfie asks, in a curious tone this time round.

"Honestly, I could add that function but I don't really see the point of it." Vetry responds.

"Ahhhh, I see and yeah, I don't really see the point of it either, anyway what do we do now?" Alfie responds in a determined tone.

"Right, once we've selected the mission, what we next have to do is draw out a possible route for the other two teams to take, taking into consideration where enemies will most likely be and how many roughly." Vetry says in a calm but clearly determined tone.

"So, take the stealth team for example, we will be figuring out the optimal route for them, but it's up to them on weather or not they take it, same applies with the frontline team, however with Hockface and Gothboy....yeah, I don't see that happening so with those two on the team, there's actually a workaround if you get to know them pretty well." Vetry Says with an awkward chuckle at the end.

"Question: What exactly do you mean by that last part?" Quinn asks, confused.

"Well, you know how those two are basically loose cannons?"

"Yeah?"

"Welllllll, that also applies to this, they don't exactly like going along the optimal route."

The two say to each other.

"Wait, how do you know this?" A red haired, spikey rebel asks.

"Well, that's actually cause those two have a tracking chip on them from one of their castle infiltrations a few years back, that was put on them by the king." Vetry says, sort of sadly but also sort of relieved at the same time.

"If that's the case then how come The King doesn't know where we are?" Quinn asks.

"I am so glad you asked, the answer is simple: I modified the chips via a surgery the two had to go through and after that/after we made sure that The King couldn't know where they are, we moved our base of operations to this house that looks just like any other so we don't stand out." Vetry responds in an extremely confident tone.

"And they've been modified so that their signal tracks back to this machine instead of one The King had." Vetry continues.

"Why couldn't you just take them out?" Quinn then asked.

"Tried to at first, but we weren't able to, well we could have theoretically but it would have killed them." Vetry responded.

"How so?" Alfie asked.

"Basically, the chips were annoyingly really deep into the body and removing it would mean taking a part their ribcages as it was beyond there which in short would render the two unable to breath and as such, it'd kill them." Vetry responded in a tone to indicate that they were thinking about something while explaining that.

"Ohhh, I see." Alfie responded.

"So, going on from that, to draw the route, all we have to do is just drag our fingers along this map and we get this little line." As Vetry draws along the map, a red line moves out from under their finger as they draw an optimal route for one of the teams, it's avoiding the king's 'guards'.

"Guessing that this is the route for the stealth team?" Quinn asked.

"Yep, you'd guess correctly, and ideally this would be done much quicker then it's taking us now." Vetry mentioned.

Before Vetry could show the frontline team's route, one of the rebels from another team runs in, while they do have a facemask and eyepatch on.

"Guys, emergency, come outside, quick." The rebel said in a massive panic, after they finish saying that, everyone runs out of the room and finds themselves outside, they notice everyone looking in the sky so everyone else follows suit and they see a bunch of human like figures flying all over the placer, however they're going too quickly to be seen properly, so there's no way to tel what they actually look like.

"How and who the hell did this?" Hockface asks.

"Well, I think I know the who..." Jacob responds.

"But you're not gonna like it." He continued.

"The King." He finished, all the time while speaking in a worried tone.

"But why? And how?" Gothboy asks, not sure weather or not she should believe Jacob.

"I don't know the how but in regards to the why: Not too long before Me, Alfie and Riley escaped, there were rumours going around that we are all going to get replaced, if those rumours are true then those things flying are our replacements." Jacob continues in a very concerned tone.

"Do you mean like he was going to fire all the human guards?" Hockface asks.

"That would be the lucky option but I honestly very highly doubt it, mostly due to well...you know what he's like." Jacob responded.

"And if you are who I think you are....you're the only one who can get through..." He says that under his breath, so no-one can hear.

"Did you say anything?" Hockface asks, confused.

"Outside of my explanation just now, nope." Jacob responded, not flustering as he knew that question was going to be asked.

"I see, well, what now? There's no telling what those things can do." Gothboy says, worridly.

"Vetry, did your team get any of the routes figured out?" Hockface asks.

"Yeah, we got the stealth team route figured out, you want them to continue as planned and scout out the castle hoping to find an entrance?" Vetry asked.

"Yeah, Stealth team, i'm assuming you have your routes on your devices ready to go?" Hockface asks.

They all look at their stuff and every single one of them has the same route on it, as if on cue, all of them nod in unison.

"Right then, continue with your mission, the rest of us are gonna stay inside, oh one more thing before you do: If you're able to find anything out about those flying things, note them down and report your findings back to us." Hockface said in a slightly worried but determined tone.

"Yes Ma'am." The stealth team replied, after which they run in different directions, as to not call attention to themselves, meanwhile all the others go back in.

Vetry and Alfie walk into the living room while the other rebels just go into other rooms to do their own things.

"Vetry, i've been wondering, is that your birth name or a nickname? I apologise if that's too personal." Alfie asks in a calm and comforting tone.

"Nah, it's ok, I may as well say where it came from, since it's not my birth name, I say what that is later." They take a deep breath and start talking...

"Before I joined the rebellion, I was a vet and ever since I was a kid, I loved taking care of animals and bringing them back to life...even if I was bullied for it." They said in a sad tone.

"Vetry..." Alfie says to himself.

"In school, people often liked to pick on me, because of my face and these stickers." They point to the animal and star stickers on their face.

"Have those been on your whole life?" Alfie asked.

"No, well not these ones specifically, usually I have to change them once or twice a month, it can be a pain but I like it." Vetry responded.

"I'm not one to judge, plus I think it looks cute on you."

Upon hearing that, Vetry blushes but quickly regains their composure and telling their story.

"Anyway, I don't know if it was because I was physically weak or what but everytime I showed empathy and kindness towards something, I was always picked on and bullied." Vetry responded.

"Yep, that's right and I couldn't stand for it anytime I saw it." That voice sounds familiar to the two and it catches them off guard, when they look at the door, they notice Gothboy walking in, saying that.

"What do you mean?" Alfie asks.

"What, you didn't think i'd protect my sis?" Gothboy asks in a joking tone to Alfie.

Hearing that catches Alfie off guard.

"You two are sisters?" He asks in surprise.

They both nod, Vetry nods rather shyly while Gothboy nods with confidence.

"Yeah, we're sisters by blood, not just bond and I will do anything to project my sis." Gothboy says with determination.

"Whenever I saw Vetry here being bullied at school, I knew I just couldn't stand back and not do anything, so despite it getting me suspended multiple times and even expelled once, it was worth it, just to see them safe." Gothboy responds.

"Wait, back up: You were suspended and expelled for protecting family from bullies? I surely hope they got much worse." Alfie says, slightly annoyed after hearing how Vetry was treated.

"Sadly, nothing happened to them, even after I tried to explain, they wouldn't listen because they only cared about their image as those bullies were also the best performing students in the school." Vetry responds with sadness.

"Despite that though, Vetty here never gave up on their dreams which makes her that much stronger then all of those bullies combined." Gothboy replies in a very proud tone.

"After that school, I made a whole bunch of new friends and even met Science Lab and we immediately hit it off." Vetry replied.

"I remember how excited you were when you said you finally met someone decent Vetty." Gothboy replied happily.

"Yeah and I also remember you sorta giving him a warning." Vetry responded in a tsundere like tone.

"Hey, that was only to protect you, i've seen your heart get broken waaaaaay too many times." Gothboy responded.

Without saying anything, Vetry hugs Gothboy and she doesn't retaliate, instead she returns the hug.

"Anyways, not long after I left school for good, I continued to follow my dreams of helping sick animals and as such, I volunteered at a vet which wasn't actually that far from where we are now and well, until this whole situation kicked off 4 years ago and ever since hockface found me and Gothboy fending on our own and fighting to survive, she invited us to the just then forming Blood Renegades." Vetry said while they're hugging Gothboy.

"I see, it makes sense as to why you two are so high ranking then." Alfie responded.

"Yep." They both said.

Meanwhile, by the castle the stealth team have split into two halves, one scouting the north of the castle, hoping to find something while the other scouts the sout with the same objective and while it seems like they might not find something, one of the south team rebels comes out of a sewer pipe right next to the north team rebels.

That rebel has really dirty camouflage clothes, their mask is similar to a masquerade mask, however it goes down their entire face when needed but it can retract as it does so when they get out of the sewer, and a bit of green can be seen under the shit that's on their hair.

"Hey, how's it going?" The rebel says while leaning out of the pipe.

"Wha- Phantom, what are you doing there?" Gasmask asks in shock.

"I saw a pipe and I got curious as to if there's any way in from here." Phantom replies.

"Well, did you get anything?" Gasmask asked.

"Yes but you're not gonna like it, pluuuuuuuuuuuuuuuus, it's not exactly the most ideal way in...Up through the toilets." Phantom asked.

"So, that's why you're covered in shit?" A different rebel asks.

"Yep, pretty much and yes, I plan to have a bath when we get back" Phantom replied.

"Good, I was gonna make you do so if you refused anyway." Gasmask said sternly.

"Phantom come in, phantom, any luck on your end? Over" A voice comes from Phantom's walkie-talkie, as soon as they hear that, they take it out and speak.

"Yes and no, depending on what your definition of luck is. Over" Phantom responded

"Well, yes I did find a way in but I don't recommend it unless you wanna smell like shit. Over" They continued.

"Gotcha. Over" The Walkie-talkie goes silent and Phantom goes back into the pipe.

The north side rebels continue scouting and aren't able to find anything, the same goes for the southside so once all of them have confirmed it, they all head back to the base; once there, every rebel except for one goes into the meeting room.

"So, that's every...wait, where's Phantom?" Hockface asks.

"They needed a bath...badly, so they won't be joining us for this meeting." Gasmask replied.

"I see, I can excuse them missing the meeting this once then." Hockface said.

"Anyway stealth team, do you have any updates for us?" She asked kindly.

"Actually yeah, we did figure out a route into the castle, well to be more specific; Phantom figured it out." Gasmask said.

"Oh? Go on?" Gothboy replied.

"A sewer pipe, which by extension, them figuring that out is also the reason why they're currently having a bath." Gasmask responded.

"Let me guess, it was full of shit?" Gothboy replied with a very cocky and proud smirk on her face.

As if on cue, everyone facepalms at the joke they all knew were coming but still walked into.

"Worth it." Gothboy said with the same cocky and proud smirk on her face.

"Aaaaanywaaaaaay, anyone find any other possible routes in for our infiltration in around a month?" Hockface asked.

"Nope." Gasmask responded.

"I see, well we still need to keep both stealth and guns blazing options avilable." Hockface mentioned.

"Well, if there's nothing else then that will conclude this meeting." Hockface says but as they start to go out, the big TV that's usually used for mapping routes and strategies for if the machine in Vetry's area wasn't working turns on and on it, a live broadcast with the country's flag comes on, just as the broadcast comes on, Phantom walks in fully clothed and dried after their bath.

Unlike the others who are still in their uniforms, Phantom is in some wholesome pyjamas with cute puppies and kittens on them.

"Wait, what's happening?" Phantom asks curiously.

"No idea, guess we've just gotta wait." Gothboy replied.

A few minutes later, the flag goes away and The King is on screen, behind him is a shadowy area with a figure that can be seen in it.

"Greetings Blood Renegades, I do hope you're all doing fine this fine evening, I am aware of your little stealth mission you performed earlier today, oh it wasn't any of the team's fault that I was aware, oh no, they did an excellent job...oh who am I kidding, it was whoever climbed through the pipe, yeah...I hope you had a bath buddy cause you'd need one." The king says rather condescendingly.

"Anyway, time for the whole reason why I even have you all watching me right now, Oooo, I feel famous: You may have noticed my new robots flying around lately and the stealth team may have noticed a lack of human guards." The king continued.

"Yeah, that did strike me as a bit odd but I just naturally assumed they were swapping." Gasmask says.

"Well, there's a very good reason for that actually: I killed them all, well all except the three that escaped from me." The king continued.

"The bastard, I know they were our enemies but he'd kill his own?" Hockface says, starting to sound pissed.

"And you may be wondering why I did that, well don't let me explain, allow the inventor of the robots to explain in my place." The King steps to one side and the shadowy figure comes out; they have red messy hair, black glasses, an evil smile on their face as well as red eyes, their clothes are a full suit, and instead of a regular tie, the person has a continental tie.

"Greetings Blood Renegades, those robots flying all over Edalbire are all made by me, with His Majesty's input and feedback." The voice sounds familiar to the rebels.

"And I fully agree with his reasoning for wanting robotic guards instead of human guards, however while I have been given permission to share it, I am choosing not to, just to keep you all in suspense, I assume you understand Your Majesty?" The person said in a calm but very clearly evil tone along with the evil smirk on their face.

"Oooo, keeping the rebels in suspense? I like that." The king says off screen.

"Anyway, before I go for now, there is just one more thing I would like to tell every single one of you Blood Renegades: Don't bother running, don't bother trying to hide, don't even bother coming to the castle because I know where your base is and as such....your days are now officially numbered, goodbye." The figure steps back into the shadows and the king comes into the view of the camera.

"Oooooo, ominous, anyway, you heard my new assistant BR, your days are numbered, so start writing your last will and testaments, the sooner the better actually." The broadcast shuts off after that.

All the rebels are in shock, not one can even say bring up the strength to say anything, and for a few minutes, everything is silent until it's broken by Gasmask.

"How does that person know where we're based?" She asked, in a rather worried tone.

"Surely it's a prank right?" Quinn asked, same tone.

"If that's who I think it is then, it's no prank and our days truly are numbered unless we act quickly..." Hockface says.

"Well then? Who is it?" Everyone asks at the same time.

"The king's new assistant is..."

Chapter 6: Receive and Turn You Part 2

Henry is leaning over the weapons, crying, while the hooded figure is just standing in the shadows, whoever they are, they clearly knew something...or at the very least, more then they let on and somehow, they seemed to know Henry but how? All these thoughts and more were flying in his head at a million MPH but he didn't have time to think about this, so Science Lab managed to somehow put them to one side and start working on the blueprints the king gave him, including a rather unique one that was very different to the weapons that he had been asked to make, but how different? Only time would tell.

"Heh, putting work before your own mental health? You haven't changed at all." The figure says quietly, it's in a volume that Science lab can't hear, or if he could, he ignored it due to the work.

While Science Lab is working, The King walks in, he seems like he was going to say something but after noticing that he's in his element, he just places something on a counter nearby and leaves the room.

A few hours later, SL stops working and almost faints due to the amount he worked, out of instinct and without thinking the figure rushes out to catch him, however once they realise what they're doing it's too late and they catch him.

After catching him, the figure puts SL on a chair and gets him some water, unbeknownst to the figure however, a bit of red is coming through the hood.

"Thank you..." SL says

"You're welcome, just...don't overwork yourself...please..." The figure replied.

But wait, who is this figure exactly? And why do they care about him despite not knowing each other for long? Those questions and more were racing through SL's mind faster then a certain blue hedgehog and as such, he held his head in both his hands and started screaming, this figure definitely seemed familiar to Science Lab, but how? Not knowing this was starting to drive him crazy and he was trying his hardest not to show it.

Upon realising what's happening, the figure swallowed and takes off their hood, upon doing so SL is shown a very familiar sight and upon seeing the person, it all comes back to him.

"....M...M...Max?" He said, trying not to burst into tears.

"Yep, sorry about being secretive, I just kinda had no choice." He replied.

Not knowing what to say, Science lab just instead hugs his old boyfriend, despite being kidnapped by him on order of the king. Although being caught off guard, Max returns the hug and strokes Henry's hair the same way he used to do it back before everything started, upon being stroked like that, Henry proceeds to cry into Max's chest.

"It's ok, just let it all out Henry, you've got plenty of time." Max said in a calming tone.

Around twenty minutes went by and Henry eventually stopped crying, he rubbed his eyes then he sat down opposite Max.

After regaining his composure, Henry starts asking Max questions that were on his mind.

"Why did you become a bounty hunter?" Was Henry's first question.

"Well, initially I wanted to be a part of the rebellion but I didn't get accepted cause I failed the training and I have no interest in working for the royal guards, so I basically just took the more exciting of the two only options available to me: Be a bounty hunter who takes no sides." Max replied.

"What was the other option?" Science Lab asked in a curious tone.

"Blend in with everyday people." He replied.

"Oh right, you never really were one for blending in with the masses, makes sense then, secondly: How'd you track me down?"

"Oh I didn't, I was given the location by The King, he knows where the rebel base is." Max responded.

"Then why hasn't he attacked it yet?" Science Lab asked.

"That's actually a good question, i'm not sure myself but he most likely has a very good reason for it." Max responded.

"Yeah, I suppose..." Henry said, rather sadly.

"Hey, you ok? Wanna talk about it?" Max asked.

"I don't know, i've just got alot of thoughts racing through my head and a whole bunch of things I need to finish for the king." Henry responded.

"I see, do you want me out of your hair then?" Max asked.

"No...I have some more things I wanna ask while i'm working." Henry responded

"Gotcha, oh one thing, I don't know if you've noticed but while you were immersed in your work, The King came by and put some new clothes on the table next to your work bench." Max said.

"Oh? Thanks for letting me know." Henry said.

"If you want me to give you privacy while you get changed, I can." Max said, knowing that SL would prefer privacy.

"Yeah, please." Science Lab responded.

When Max goes back into the room, Science lab's clothes are now a full suit, with a continental tie, black glasses and the same messy red hair as before.

With awe and amazement, Max looked at Henry and said "Wow Henry, you look just as amazing as ever!"

While blushing, Henry responds with "Heh, thanks Max" Soon after saying that, he manages to regain his composure and starts working on the items again.

In a curious voice, Max asked "So, what are you working on if you don't mind me asking?"

Although he clearly wants to answer the question honestly, he can't for whatever reason and as such, Henry dodges around the question "I would say if I could."

With confusion, Max looks to Science Lab "Huh? What do you mean?"

"I just don't...want to talk about it right now, if that's ok."

Upon hearing that, Max drops the topic, he knew that when Henry got like this, it'll be best to leave him alone and as such, he leaves the room, leaving Henry to get on with his work, however before leaving the room, Max puts his hood back on. "I'll see you later".

After giving Henry a quick hug and leaving the room, Max makes his way to the throne room, making sure that his identity is hidden, after entering, he clears his throat to make his presence known.

Upon hearing that, the king turns around and notices Max has entered the room "Ah, Ghost, welcome back."

Putting on a serious voice, Max/Ghost speaks. "I have done what you asked Your Highness, now your end of the bargain, my payment please." Ghost was being serious, he wasn't playing around, at all.

However despite promising the money, The king had other ideas and told Ghost no.

He clearly wasn't expecting that so because of that, Ghost is very surprised and pissed when they speak. "What do you mean? This is a two way street, you don't back out on the payment."

"Well too bad, because that's exactly what I did, GUARDS!!!!!"

After shouting that, robotic footsteps can be heard approaching and a few seconds later, two robotic arms grab Ghost from the shadows and a robotic voice can be heard. "**WHAT WOULD YOU LIKE US TO DO WITH HIM, MASTER?**"

In response to that question, The King turns back around and speaks in a serious tone again "Dispose of him, anyway you see fit."

After getting the command, the robots walk away with Ghost and a few minutes later, they throw him out of the castle and into the water nearby, thus making his clothes all wet, however he doesn't seem to care as he gets up and walks away from the castle, while walking however he goes into thought.

'Huh, surprised I wasn't executed but damnit, I need to get back in there and get my payment and well...to be able to talk to Henry again, I know that the rebellion is planning a siege on the castle but I don't know when that's going to happen and after failing, there's no way they'll let me back in and if they find out that I was the one who kidnapped their scientist for that Scrooge then i'm dead meat, no two ways round it...looks like i'm well and truly on my own...heh, kinda like the start of a story but sadly, this is no story, it's reality.'

While walking aimlessly, a bunch of rebels drive by really quickly, seeming like they're coming back from their last mission.

'Heh, could have been me in one of those cars but well, it's what happened really and to be perfectly honest I much prefer being down the middle....well, most of the time when clients pay, however clients like him I hate, I don't care about their status, if they hired me then they need to be ready to pay...now, how do I do this? Regicide is out of the question...'

While remaining in thought, Ghost keeps on walking and meanwhile back in the castle's workshop room, the King walks in as SL finishes work on the final robot, "Ah your highness, great timing, I just finished constructing the final bot you asked me to make."

The King's face goes from one of anger to one of delight. "Sweet and I see you got the uniform I gave you on, oh idea, wanna go and do something that's really gonna spook the rebellion?"

Henry looks over with curiosity in his voice "Just what do you mean?"

"Follow me." Both Henry and The King leave the room, soon after they go to a room that has a camera set up. Before that however, the two take five of the robots to the front of the castle and activate them, once they're activated, they start flying all over Edalbire.

While walking down to the room, Henry speaks "I've been wondering, what is the reason why you want robotic guards rather then human ones?"

Surprisingly, the King doesn't respond in a pissed tone, instead he's more then willing to answer the question: "Easy, robotic guards won't betray me at all unlike the human ones which did...more then once."

"I see and if you don't mind me asking, where are the human ones now?"

With no resistance or restraint, the King responds with "Executed."

"Oh...."

"Oh by the way, you're more then welcome to tell the rebels the reason for this or you don't have to, your choice."

"Okey doke."

After that conversation, they arrive to the room with the camera

The king starts speaking "Right, just stand infront of the camera."

"Actually, what if I go into the shadows and slowly walk forwards when you need me to reveal myself?"

"Oh? That would work brilliantly."

After that little interaction, the two get the broadcast set up and the King goes infront of the camrea.

In a rather condesending tone, he speaks to the camera "Greetings Blood Renegades, I do hope you're all doing fine this fine evening, I am aware of your little stealth mission you performed earlier today, oh it wasn't any of the team's fault that I was aware, oh no, they did an excellent job...oh who am I kidding, it was whoever climbed through the pipe, yeah...I hope you had a bath buddy cause you'd need one."

"Anyway, time for the whole reason why I even have you all watching me right now, Oooo, I feel famous: You may have noticed my new robots flying around lately and the stealth team may have noticed a lack of human guards."

"Well, there's a very good reason for that actually: I killed them all, well all except the three that escaped from me." The king continued.

"And you may be wondering why I did that, well don't let me explain, allow the inventor of the robots to explain in my place." The King steps to one side and Henry in his new suit walks infront of the camera with a sinister smile on his face

"Greetings Blood Renegades, those robots flying all over Edalbire are all made by me, with His Majesty's input and feedback."

"And I fully agree with his reasoning for wanting robotic guards instead of human guards, however while I have been given permission to share it, I am choosing not to, just to keep you all in suspense, I assume you understand Your Majesty?"

"Oooo, keeping the rebels in suspense? I like that." The king says off screen.

"Anyway, before I go for now, there is just one more thing I would like to tell every single one of you Blood Renegades: Don't bother running, don't bother trying to hide, don't even bother coming to the castle because I know where your base is and as such....your days are now officially numbered, goodbye."

"Oooooo, ominous, anyway, you heard my new assistant BR, your days are numbered, so start writing your last will and testaments, the sooner the better actually." The broadcast shuts off after that.

Stepping out of the shadows and looking at the King, Science lab speaks to him. "So, do you need me for anything else your highness?"

"Nope, go back to your lab and continue the work, i'll summon you later if I need anything."

"Very well."

After that, Science Lab starts walking out of the room and just walks back into his room, expecting to find Max there, however once he arrives, he doesn't see him anywhere, knowing that The King would be pissed if he were to ask, Science Lab instead closes and locks the door from the inside of the lab, pulls out a phone and starts ringing someone.

A few minutes after dialing, someone picks up.

The other person's voice sounds distorted "Hello?"

Once the other person picks up, he starts speaking "GB, this is SL, is SW and V with you?"

"Nice, listen, B has gone missing, I can't find them here, are they where you are by any chance?"

"......"

"I see...Well, i'll try phoning them, hope they pick up....gotcha, will do, well then...take care GB"

After saying that, he puts the phone down and calls a different number but no answer from it, despite that however it did ring so SL puts the phone back in his pocket, hoping it rings with B on the other end.

Hours pass, soon days pass, soon even a week passes and not once did he get a call from B and now as such, he ends up being extremly worried, to the point where one night, he sneaks out the castle looking for them.

Edalbire was a very different place at night, instead of just walking around freely, Henry had to sneak around and be stealthy, he knows that if he's caught out at night, he's dead, no two ways round it, however for some reason, he's taking the risk just for one person, he spends most of the night looking around Edalbire but to no avail, however that's because he only had the time to search and skulk around one small area of the country's capital of Tehctar.

Once he looked at his watch and noticed that it was nearly 4AM, he skulked back to the castle as quickly as he could, making sure to avoid the guard bots along the way and as such, he is able to make it in time so he sets his alarm for 7AM, gets into his room and climbs into bed and goes to sleep.

Just under two hours later, Henry wakes up after hearing his alarm go off, leaves his room and goes to a kitchen to make himself breakfast, after he's all tidied up and ready to begin the day, he goes back to his lab in the castle, the day is like any other day he's lived there: Test weapons he made, if they're good enough, make more and so on...weirdly, he starts thinking about his time in the rebellion and how it's a bit too similar to that.

However unlike any other day, this day...was one that was rather eventful because he had finished a weapon The King had been working on for some time now: The Sonic Soundwave Disrupter...or the SSD.

As soon as it's complete, he invites The King into the lab but this time, he's accompanied by a hovering monitor that's following him with a shadowy person on the screen, keeping their identity a secret for obvious reasons.

Upon hearing the two come in, Henry starts to speak "Ah, Your Highness, welcome, who is this may i ask?"

The person speaks instead of The King and it's clear that they're using a voice disrupter "No, you may not know who I am, now speak! What does this thing Seth told me about do and how will it help stop the rebellion uprising?"

"Well you see whatever your name is, the Sonic Soundwave Disrupter, or SSD for short is a special weapon that can completely incapacitate anyone with sounds that only the people in the general area can hear and depending on the serverity of things, it can last between 30 seconds to two minutes, leaving ourside with plenty of time to gain the upper hand on the rebellion when they inevitably raid."

"Following on from that, it also has three modes, by default it's set to mode two which has enough range to cover around five-ten miles, mode three is able to cover this entire city and a bit beyond that but right now, it's defaulted to mode two cause we shouldn't need to use mode three and mode one-"

The voice cuts Henry off "Got the gist of it, any chance of a demonstration?"

"Sure, let me just set to mode one real quick."

While he's doing that, the voice speaks to The King. "Seth! Go to the middle of the room and stay there, I want to see this thing in action."

Weirdly scared, which is very unusal for him, Seth moves to the centre of the room after everything is moved out of the way, as soon as they're both ready, Henry aims the gun at Seth and activates it, at which point he's trying really hard not to scream in pain as it's somehow hurting him, after ten seconds, Henry deactivates it and meanwhile Seth is on the ground with his hands to his head, still trying not to scream.

"Interesting and you say that modes two and three have bigger area zones?"

"Yep, tested it myself in a simulator so I can confirm."

"I see and I can see how this would take care of the rebellion but how about... *The agency*"

Upon hearing those two words at the end, Henry is taken aback, he wasn't expecting this voice to know about that, so how did they know about it and what's their deal? He wanted to ask however the vibes the figure gave off are ones that basically say not to ask stuff like that and as such, he keeps his mouth shut.

The figure is starting to get impatient "Well?"

"I'm sorry but I have no idea who 'The Agency' are"

While that was in a desperate attempt to lie, Henry was somehow able to say that with a straight face and whatever his tell is; it clearly wasn't visible, at least, not to the naked eye and after hearing that, the figure decides to leave it alone.

"Very well then, i'll leave you to clear up this mess as i'll take my leave."

After saying that, the figure leaves the room via their monitor and once gone, Henry goes to the king and helps him up who shoves him out of the way, instead of saying anything, he leaves the room pissed off, most likely going to have a few words with that figure.

In the throne room, the same figure from before is on a giant monitor, while Seth is pacing back and forth.

"So? How you holding up?"

Upon hearing that, Seth's face goes to extremly pissed.

"How i'm holding up? You tell my lab rat shoot me with the gun and you have the gall to ASK HOW I'M HOLDING UP?!?!?!? HOW THE FUCK DO YOU THINK I'M HOLDING UP!??!?!"

"Ah-ah-ah-ah-ah, remember what's set to happen when you talk back to me?"

"Ugh, I won't let you kill me."

"Oh I have no intentions on killing you, what with the rebellion's final plans starting to be put into effect."

"Wait, hold on a minute, what do you mean?"

"Damn, i'm surprised your so called 'lab rat' never mentioned it."

"What do you mean...?"

"Very well, I'll have to explain it; You may have noticed that lately, your bases have been going down rather rapidly because you did a crap job at guarding them."

"OI!"

"Shut it you, anyway as I was saying, the Blood Renegades have been taking down all your bases one by one and rather rapidly, they're getting ready to do their final one soon, like, next two hours soon because tomorrow guess what they plan to do."

"You're kidding me..."

"Nope, in two hours, unless you put ALL your forces to that one base, to at least slow them down, you're kinda fucked, even with your robots gaurding the castle."

"Wait, how do you know about the robots?"

"Me to know and you to find out....well, if you survive that is."

"If I survive...what does that mean?"

"Oh, didn't I tell you? The Agency has also been keeping dibs on your actions and the UN are now they're getting ready to send MI6 after you to arrest you and then hold a public trial."

"How do you even know all this? Are you bullshitting me?"

"I may be and I may not be, wheather or not you believe me is entierly up to you."

"Ugh..."

"Well anyway, the thing I said about the rebellion's plans; yeah, that bit is 100% true so I recommend you think about it but don't spend too long; remember, you've only got two hours so you better decide what you're gonna do and quickly."

After the figure hangs up, Seth goes over to a microphone and presses a button.

"East side robots, go to the co-ordinates i'm about to send to you, west side robots come back to the castle and guard it, and east side robots, once you've killed the rebels, you are to come back here and join the west side robots in guarding the place."

All at once, the robots respond in a robotic voice.

"**ROGER!**"

After saying that, he goes over to a window.

"So, Hope...if you are who I think you are then...we're gonna meet again and very soon...."

Meanwhile in the lab, Henry finished working and as such, he looked at his watch however, he notices just how much time has passed since he woke up and seeing that it's gone 8 again, he sneaks out the room and goes to look for Ghost again.

Rather then going the same route he took last night, he goes the opposite route, after a whole bunch of sneaking around and avoiding eventually is able to find someone, however with it being the middle of the night, he cautiously approaches the figure, however they turn around and : immediately, recognises who it is and as such, the two hug.

After the hug however, Henry slaps Max "Where the hell were you? You got everyone else worried."

Max rubs the side of their face "Firstly: I deserved that and secondly: I got kicked out of the castle by The King cause he refused to pay me."

Henry's looks turns from one of relived but slightly annoyed to one of confusion "Pay you, what do you mean?"

"Promse not to kill me if I tell you?"

"I promise."

Max sighs then gulps

"He commissioned me to kidnap you."

Instead of saying anything, Henry just hugs Max.

"You're...not pissed or anything?"

"Nuh-uh, I know your job outside the agency, I knew that eventually something like that would happen, i'm just glad that it was you who did it and not someone else."

Hearing that completely surprises Max, they were fully expecting Henry to absolutely lose it, however he didn't and in response, Max just returns the hug and after a few minutes, the two stare into the distance.

"When is the date?"

"What date?"

"The day the rebellion intends to kick the revolution into high gear?"

"Oh...tomorrow."

"How about *The Agency*?"

"What about them?"

"Have you kept in contact with them?"

"No, like we were told not to."

"Good, I don't want to think what *she'd* do if *she* found out that someone on the team contacted them for a non important reason."

"Yeah, same."

The two stare off into the distance where Rebellion vehciles are seen in the distance driving really fast to a destination.

Chapter 7: The Night Before The Fall of Edalbire Part 1

Everyone is standing in the breifing room, looking at Hockface after what she just said, she also stands there and sighs, knowing full well that what she's about to say could very well send the entire rebellion into chaos, however she braces herself... "Science Lab..."

Just as she feared, everyone in the rebellion was talking over each other and shouting, no-one could get a word in, not even Gothboy or hockface shouting at everyone to tell them to be quiet works and as such, Gasmask flips a switch that's only intended to be used against intruders and fires some sleeping gas that puts everyone except her to sleep.

She starts thinking to herself 'Oh right....oops...' Clearly not thinking it through, she stops the sleeping gas and just sits down in another room looking at the same photo from before, getting lost in thought.

'I miss you all, I know *you* got out of here but...where did you go? I never saw you at HQ once and yet you said you went there...' Some tears start going down Gasmask's face but before she can properly let them out, she notices people start to wake up so she wipes her eyes and puts on a brave face, even though deep down, she's really emotional right now.

As people slowly wake up, she hides the photo in her jacket pocket and makes up an excuse for why everyone was out of it.

"Oh, there was an intruder and I took them down to the interrogation room."

Gothboy starts walking out of the room with the intent to interrogate this person, however as she goes past Gasmask, she grabs her arm and whispers.

"Meet me outside in ten minutes, there is no-one new down in that room."

She nods and leaves the room as to not raise the suspicions of anyone who is in the room, meanwhile Hockface looks at the two and confused.

"What was that about So- Gasmask?"

"Oh, I just needed to tell Gothboy something."

"Uhuh? And it couldn't have waited until after she was done?"

"Nope."

"I see..."

Altho clearly getting suspicious of Gasmask, Hockface knows that she's also been guilty of doing stuff like that so, she can't exactly stay suspicious for long.

After the meeting had concluded, everyone else started to walk out the room, meanwhile Hockface was in deep thought.

'How could he though...Plus wouldn't he take Proto with him?'

Proto beeps worridly on Hockface's shoulder.

"I'm worried too lil guy."

'I wonder...did he even go willingly? I recall him once saying that he would always take Proto with him wherever he went...maybe i'm thinking too much into this...I don't know...'

She sighs and walks out of the room, meanwhile keeping Proto on her shoulder.

Outside the base, Gasmask sits on a rebel car, while Gothboy sits on the one next to it.

"So, what'cha want to talk to me about?"

"It's about this."

Gasmask pulls out the photo from before and points to the boy.

"Sapphire? What about him?"

"When I last spoke to him, he said that he was assigned to this operation but I haven't seen or heard from him since the operation started."

"Hmmm, that's definitely weird, do the others know about this?"

"Can't inform M or H for obvious reasons and I need to somehow get A and V in the same room together."

"What do you mean? A and V are usually always in the same room."

Instead of responding, Gasmask just looks confused.

"Yeah, those two are the two main mission strategists, so they're constantly in the same room."

"Oh, when did that happen?"

"Not too long ago actually"

"I see."

After that conversation is finished, Gothboy walks in first, a few minutes after she goes in, Gasmask follows suit as to not raise any suspicions from Hockface, then again...why are they trying so hard to avoid her?

Despite that, after a few minutes of walking and intentionally trying to avoid the rebel leader, Gasmask also arrives at the strategy room where Alfie, Vetry and Gothboy are all waiting for her.

Alfie is the first one to speak.

"Ah good, you're, anyways, you two wanted to tell us something?"

They both explain what they talked about before going down there.

A few minutes of silence is in the room before Vetry breaks it.

"I see...I hope he's all right...It must suck now knowing where he is, espically since he's your brother."

One of the three looks down at the floor, with a bit of sadness in their eyes.

"Yeah...it is, I know we hadn't known each other for too long but I miss him already."

The other two agree with the missing part, however those two had known Sapphire for longer then his brother somehow.

Gasmask then speaks up.

"Wait, Vetry and Alfie, couldn't you hack into CF servers and get Sapphire's latest mission details?"

Vetry responds while crossing their arms.

"Oh we wish, but no, if that was possible, it would have been the first thing we did after you told us what's been going on with Sapphire."

"I see, anyway Gothboy, we should head back up before the others start to get suspicious."

She agrees and the two walk out of the room, separately again, soon after, both of them are back in the living space with Gothboy having a laptop out and working on something.

"So, how's it coming along Gothboy?"

Hockface asks that while she's walking into the room.

"Pretty well actually, the country and the King ain't gonna know what's boutta hit it."

"Boutta?"

"Yeah, it's almost ready to go, just gotta add a few more finishing touches, infact depending on how long it takes to render and export, we may be able to have this thing ready to go either tonight or tomorrow."

Hockface's eyes light up with excitement.

"So you're basically saying that our plan is almost ready to be put into action?"

"Yep, although I do want everyone's opinions on it first once it's ready so, if you could call everyone into the meeting room in around....maybe an hour or so I can show it off there."

"Gotcha, will do."

"Sweet, If it's ready before then, i'll let you know."

"Gotcha."

After that conversation, Hockface walks out of the room and out of earshot.

"Huh? Whatcha working on C?"

"A little 'advertisement' for the rebellion."

As Gothboy says the word "Advertisement", she does it in air quotes which Gasmask quickly picked up as to her having some sort of ultior motive/is lying about it advertising the rebellion.

"Oooo, can I see?"

Gasmask asked with excitement in her eyes and voice.

"Not yet S, I wanna show this to everyone at the same time."

"Gotcha."

Gasmask starts playing a video game to pass the time while Gothboy is working on the video.

'Up, down, up, down, up, down, up, down, Chu, Chu, Chu." The sounds coming out of the TV, Gothboy also finds herself vibing to the music while working on the editing.

Fourty-five minutes later, Gothboy is ready to show the others and as such, she calls Hockface who then proceeds to call a meeting back in the briefing room.

Once everyone is there, Gothboy connects her laptop to the projector and some speakers at which point, the video starts to play:

On the video there are silhouettes of the members of the rebellion on a dark red background with voiceover provided by multiple members and intense final confrontation music in the background.

A few minutes later, the video ends and the entire room starts cheering, at which point, Gothboy takes that as a sign that it's ready; at which point she leaves the room to get the process started, meanwhile Hockface takes the rebels in the room through the briefing of the final mission before the final operation began to take over the throne, hell the country was already on edge, it just needed one little push to send it into complete chaos and this video would do exactly that.

"Right, we learnt that The King still has one base left for his robots, we need to destroy it ASAP so which team would be the most effective at that?"

Each rebel raises their hand.

"Ok....should have known that, that wasn't gonna work, well usually I would just send Gothboy on her own due to her expertise with explosive weapons but that's a no-go this time cause as we all know, she's pre-occupied, however anyone else here good with explosives?"

Two rebels from two different teams raise their hands.

"Ok, perfect, which teams are you two on?"

"Frontline"

"Stealth"

"Right, well do you want me and Gasmask to come with or are you both fine on your own?"

The two converse and agree to Hockface and Gasmask joining them on the mission since those two had never done anything like that before, also not wanting to stand out, the two had tidy brunette hair and wore generic looking clothes.

"Perfect, get changed and meet us at the garage in half an hour, the rest of you, best to get to bed early tomorrow and be up at midnight the next day; we've all got a big day ahead of us then and that's when we begin."

The time passes and the four are there, sitting in a gar with Gasmask in the drivers seat, Hockface in the front passenger seat and the two rebels who volunteered in the backseat; to avoid having their identity seen, the two in the back seat also have anonymous masks on.

Outside, it's pitch black, night time just rolled in and people are driving back and fourth on the busy road, both the headlights of the car and street lamps on the road have lit up the roads, during the way there Hockface starts talking.

"Right, let's go over the plan, firstly you two will be scouting out the area for us as well as deactivating any alarms that might be there and armed, after those two have done their job, they come back into the car and we plant the explosives that are in the boot all over the base at which point, we use the rocket launcher on the floor of the back of the car to blow it up, once we're a safe distance away, any questions?"

One of the two rebels has a question about if there's a button to blow up the explosives.

"Yeah, i've got that button in my pocket and don't worry, they're not armed right now, we won't be arming them until we're a safe distance away."

The two nod in understanding.

"Right, you both ready for this?"

They nod again.

"Sweet, get ready, we're almost there."

A few minutes later, the car pulls up to the base and once parked, Gasmask turns off the engine and lights after that, the two leave the the car and turn on their suit flash lights in order to not be seen.

The base is pitch black so all that can be seen while they're inside are the metallic walls and floor, at which point the two enter a split so they agree to go opposite directions, Gasmask doesn't come across anything of note, except a control panel which after turning on, activates...something...

Gasmask can hear the sounds of machine engines activating; she points her flashlight towards the sounds in which she can see through the window:

The King's robots being assembled and shipped off to the castle, upon realising this, Gasmask immediately presses the button again which powers down the machine, after which, she finds where the alarm is in the area and, goes to deactivate it.

However, before she can deactivate it, Gasmask has to play a little memory game as the buttons on a giant board light up in the order she needs to press them:

Red

White

Sapphire

Gold

Violet

She presses the buttons, however almost misses a few of them; there's no telling how many attempts she'd have but one thing is for sure: If she did miss them enough times, an alarm would obviously go off, thus alerting Seth to the current going ons inside this base/factory.

Meanwhile on the other side of the base, the first anonymous rebel is sneaking around with their flashlight helmet on and come across a similar control panel to the one Gasmask was just at, however unlike Gasmask who just pressed the first button as soon as she saw it, the rebel looks all around and sees the same room Gasmask just saw.

Upon seeing that, they inspect the control panel and notice the buttons, they press the button with an alarm icon and much to their surprise, it does not activate an alarm; instead it brings up a similar board to the one that Gasmask saw and as such, they have to play the same game but this time round, the colours are different:

Blue

Black

Ruby

Silver

Scarlet

The rebel presses the buttons in the order that they appeared in...after failing once on Black then once on Silver, suddenly a loud voice booms through the building.

"SYSTEMS DEACTIVATED. SHUTTING DOWN BOT CREATION FACILITY."

After hearing that, both Gasmask and the rebel meet outside and they talk about what they both had to do, after they get to the car, the two let Hockface and the other rebel know that it's ok for them to go in.

As Gasmask and the other rebel are getting into the car, Hockface and the other anonymous rebel leave and enter the facility, soon after they come up to the same split that Gasmask and her rebel ally came to.

Hockface is the one to break the ice "So, wanna split up or stick together?"

"Split up, it'll be easier to cover more ground."

"Couldn't agree more."

The two get to their respective control panels and start planting the explosives and arming them, ready to go off as soon as the button in Hockface's jacket has been pressed, slowly but surely, the two keep planting the explosives all over the base....just to make doubly sure, after around an hour, they eventually finish up and plant the last few explosives on the outside corners of the factory.

As soon as those have been planted and armed, Hockface and the anonymous rebel head back to the car and get in; once they're in, Gasmask turns it around and starts driving away.

As soon as all four are a safe distance away, Hockface gets the button out and Gasmask parks the car.

The anonymous rebel who was with Gasmask speaks first.

"Two questions: A: What time is it and B: Should we all press it together?"

Hockface looks at her watch.

"Damn, it's getting late: 8:30PM."

Gasmask responds next

"Ooof and yeah, I think we should."

"Right, on the count of three..."

All four of them place their hands on the device and thumbs over the button itself and start counting down:

"1"

"2"

"3"

At the count of three, all of them press the button and they all see the factory blow up in the distance, with robot and building parts flying everywhere, including near the car itself.

"Think we went a little too overboard on the explosives?"

"In the immortal words of one very wise and philosophical Gothboy: 'You can never have too many explosives'"

The four of them take one last look at the factory as it goes up in flames then drive away, and start listening to the radio.

"Breaking news: Reports just in of a mysterious explosion near one of the secret factories, the cause of the explosion is unknown, but it'll be very likely to assume that these so called 'Blood Renegades' are behind it, his Royal Highness issued the following statement within the last few minutes."

"Greetings loyal subjects, as you may or may not be aware, one of my precious factories was blown up recently, for those of you who are like 'Who cares? It's just a factory', initially those would be natural assumptions, however one less of this specific type of factory means weaker security from those pesky rebels."

Hockface scoffs

"Yeah, right, those things totally don't kill indiscriminatory."

"And as such, I urge any law abiding citizen to report any possible rebels to a nearby security bot, they'll take it from there and if they turn out to be a rebel then they'll be dealt with accordingly, however if not then they'll be put back in society, I thank you for your time and co-operation, especially now that I am on my own due to the unfortunate passing of my new colleague."

"Oh and Blood Renegades, I know what you're planning and I just have one thing to say: Do...Your....Worst!!!!"

"Those words were just delivered by the His Royal Highness not fifteen minutes ago and strong words there for the rebellion, just how will they respond? Only time will tell, this reporter however is betting on them cowering out."

"Excuse me, what the fuck!?!?!"

Hockface sounds really shocked right now, and for good reason, Science Lab was just announced dead by His Royal Highness, as such, she turns the radio off.

"That fucking bastard killed him, I can garuntee it."

While driving, gasmask's phone vibrates in her pocket, when she gets to the garage, she parks up and turns the engine, meanwhile Hockface and the two anonymous rebels leave the vehicle, while she stays in and checks her phone...it's a text from Science lab.

"I'm safe, I faked my death, DON'T tell Hockface this until after the plan has been finished, I have already alerted CF HQ about my status and now they're aware of everything going on."

"If the plan fails, meet me three miles out of the border tomorrow night at 11PM, we can reconvine at CF HQ with the others and come up with a plan there."

"I have also texted the others so they know about my situation as well, however I was unable to tell B as I still can't get a hold of them and not gonna lie. I'm starting to get worried."

A second text appears:

"TL;DR Faked my death, don't tell Hockface, still can't contact B, so i'll see you tomorrow night."

Upon receiving those texts, Gasmask leaves the car and enters the base, at which point she's walks past both Gasmask and Gothboy and decides to head to bed to get as much rest as possible for midnight.

Meanwhile back in the briefing room, Hockface and Gothboy are going through the video together.

"So, we're ready for this now?"

"Yep, the video is 100% finished, I just want your opinion on it."

"I see but why mine alone?"

"Why else? You're our leader, I wouldn't want to do show this off without getting the green light from you first."

"I see, Gothboy, I trust you enough to use your own intuition but I am glad that you came to me first."

They finish watching it.

"So? Whatcha think?"

"It's perfect, we will send this at exactly midnight, which means that we have 2 ½ hours to spare, i'll go send out an announcement to the public saying to stay up and expect something then."

"Gotcha, what should I do?"

"Whatever, I don't really mind but I do need you awake for midnight so we can send it off."

"Alrighty, i'll probably just go for a walk then."

"Eh? That's not like you."

"I know but I wanna clear my mind, espically with what happened earlier and the death of Science Lab."

"How'd you know about that?"

"You're forgetting Hockey, we can access the news here as well."

"Oh right, anyways, enjoy your walk."

"I will"

And with that, Gothboy leaves the rebel base and just starts walking mindlessly, however once she's enough distance away, she gets a call from an unknown number, her gut tells her to block it, she answers it, as there's a chance that it may be Science Lab calling from a burner phone in order to keep hidden.

"Hello?"

A familiar voice comes through the other end; It's not Science Lab's but instead, it's Bounty's voice, upon hearing that, Gothboy breaths a sigh of relief.

"Where have you been Bounty, we've been worried sick, we thought you died."

"Heh, honestly, i've been wanting some time alone so I just kept my phone turned off, guess I should have updated you all."

"Ya think? Anyways, i'm glad you're safe."

"Oh, I also got the text from Science Lab as well, glad to hear that he's safe."

"100% agreed, so whatcha gonna do now?"

"Depends, does the rebellion have anything planned in retaliation for what The King said?"

"Yep."

"In that case, i'm gonna stick back and watch the fireworks from a safe space, I got what I needed from The King...even if he doesn't know it's missing juuuuuuuust yet."

"What'd you get?"

"Just my payment, that's all."

"I see...anyway, where should we meet?"

"Where Science Lab said; 3 miles out of the border, meet us two there at 11PM tomorrow."

"Ok, gotcha, see you then."

Gothboy puts the phone down and continues walking to clear her mind for a bit, after a little bit, she looks at her watch, notices that it's 10PM then turns around and heads back to the base.

Once she gets back there and warms up, she sees Hockface watching the news on the TV.

The newsroom looks just like any other TV newsroom and the reporter is wearing smart clothing with their hair neatly layed out

"Not too long before this broadcast, the Blood Renegades making a public announcement in response to what The King said earlier."

"Revealing that they have something special planned for midnight tonight, which is just under 90 minutes from now, we'll go back to our regularly scheduled programming for an hour, see you in an hour."

The news theme plays and Hockface turns the TV off.

After the news is turned off, Gothboy goes to her laptop to double check that everything is all connected and working, she does a broadcast which makes all outside screens in Edalbire light up with the logo of the rebellion:

A silhouette of a violent looking doberman with sharp red eyes and the the words "For the truth!" going along the middle of it, with a circle going round it which inside reads: "Blood Renegades, the rebels fighting for the truth!"

When half 11 rolls around, the news comes back on with the same host as before.

"Welcome back to the news, over the last hour, a development happened in that all the electric ad boards and TVs in all major cities have been hijacked by the Blood Renegades themselves, indicating that they may have some sort of message they intend to broadcast soon, how soon? We don't know but we will be the first to update you as developments happen."

"In the meantime however, we have one of the oldest royal family members here who retired before the unfortunate passing of the previous king and queen, thanks for coming on."

The family is a friendly looking old man with a sweater/jumper, full suit trousers and smart shoes with a cane/walking stick.

"Thank you for having me, Edalbire has certainly changed alot in just a few short years."

"Indeed it has, some would say for the better, others would say for the worst, however as an ex castle guard, what's your opinion on it?"

"Well I would agree with both sides, in some ways, yes it has changed for the better and in others, it hasn't...I just wish my dear niece and nephew would get along again, I miss those days and my dear wife would be extremely disappointed in what they both have become."

"Yeah, many of us down here feel that way as well, if they could get along much like their parents did then...maybe things would be better for the whole country."

"100% agreed, although what's your opinion on those rumours that The King kicked his own sister out from the castle?"

"Those aren't rumours ma'am, that's a fact, not long after the death of their parents, he kicked out his own sister, I don't know the full specifics as to why though."

"I understand completely and if you don't want to answer my next question then we can just skip it if that's ok with you."

"Certainly."

"There are some rumours going around that the leader of the Blood Renegades is actually The King's sister, what's your opinion on that?"

"Well, I haven't heard such things and to me, that just sounds like tabloid gossip."

"I see, is there anything else you'd like to say before our interview concludes?"

"Yes."

The old man looks directly into the camera.

"Hope and Seth, if you're both watching this, please, I implore you both to try and reconcile and rule Edalbire as a loving brother and sister duo."

The old man looks back to the interviewer.

"Agreed and yet again Mr. Kingston, thank you for joining us in the studio this evening."

"It's my pleas-"

Before he could finish talking, the reporter gets a message in their ear.

"I am so sorry to cut you off there but we just got some breaking news."

"Oh go ahead."

"This just in, the screens all have a 5 minute countdown on them and with it being 11:55PM, i'm guessing that they're waiting until midnight to deliver their message and with only 5 minutes left, who knows what they have to say...stay tuned."

Chapter 8: The Night Before The Fall of Edalbire Part 2

In the King's throne room, the figure on the monitor and The King are both arguing so loud, that if some were that high up on the outside, they'd be able to hear what they're arguing about.

"WHAT DO YOU MEAN YOU DON'T KNOW WHERE YOUR LAB RAT IS!?!!?"

"EXACTLY WHAT IT SAYS, I DON'T KNOW WHERE THE FUCK HE'S GONE!!!!"

"DO YOU EVEN REALISE THE IMPLICATIONS OF THIS?!?!?! IF HE GETS BACK TO THE REBELLION, YOU'RE COMPLETELY FUCKED!!!!"

"YES, I KNOW EXACTLY WHAT THE IMPLICATIONS ARE, I'VE ALSO RULED THIS COUNTRY LONGER THAN YOU'VE BEEN THE LEADER OF CHAOS CRUSADORS SO I THINK I KNOW FAIR BIT MORE THAN YOU!!!"

"OI, DON'T TALK TO ME LIKE THAT YOU LOW-LIFE, THE ONLY REASON WHY YOU'RE NOT DEAD YET IS CAUSE I STILL NEED YOU!!!"

"THAT IS BULLSHIT AND YOU KNOW IT PURGE!!!!"

"OH YEAH? WANNA SEE HOW YOU HANDLE THE REBELLION'S UPCOMING PLANS ON YOUR OWN?!?!?!?!"

And with that, the figure, known only as Purge turns off their monitor, thus making Seth lose signal to them, he is clearly very pissed, espically due to the rebellion taking down nearly all of his bases and factories, as well as the whole country being on edge thanks to the actions by the rebellion.

Not all was lost, he still has one more factory left, however due to it being the final one, tensions are very high right now and it's painfully obvious that he is really stressed.

Not in his wildest dreams did he expect the rebellion to actually do this much damage to him; not when he had human guards/soliders and still not with the robot ones.

Alongside those as well, his lab rat has also gone missing, leaving him with many semi-complete weapons and only a handful of finished ones, including the SSWD: Sonic Soundwave Disrupter.

However, one question that played on his mind over and over and over again is: 'Just how did he escape? He shouldn't have been able to, one step outside this castle and he's dog food and yet...there aren't any body parts anywhere near it.'

He paced up and down the throne room until one of his robots entered the room.

"SIR, ONE OF US CAME BACK FROM PATROL AND FOUND OUT THAT THE REBELLION PLANS TO LAUNCH AN ATTACK ON THE FINAL FACTORY TONIGHT!"

"Why am I not surprised?"

"WHAT DO YOU WANT US TO DO?"

"Stand your grounds."

"ARE YOU SURE SIR?"

"Yes, I am sure, what are you growing some sort of soul now?"

"NO, THE GUN-100 SERIES DOES NOT HAVE SOULS, UNLIKE OUR INFERIOR 200 SERIES COUNTERPARTS"

"Good, I don't expect you to grow any morals or soul."

"I HAVE NO INTENTIONS OF EVER DOING SO."

"Good, now, activate that final factory's systems, keep it ungarded and at 20:00 tonight, turn it off and send all the newly made robots to me, along with every robot currently out on patrol, tomorrow..."

"....We **KILL** the Blood Renegades, HOWEVER you MUST bring their leader to me alive, I want to kill them myself."

"ROGER THAT SIR! RESUMING PATROL NOW!"

The robot leaves the room, leaving The King back on his own again, however the figure from before comes back.

"Heh, you really should learn how to mute yourself."

He growls very audibly, almost like a wild animal about to go after it's prey.

"Damn, temper, temper, I know you're pissed with me and quite frankly, i'm pissed with you as well but hey, we do need to work as a team, sooooooooo, yeah."

"Remind me again why you assigned yourself to me?"

"Because you're smart but you're also an idiot."

Instead of saying anything, his face changes to one that looks like it's ready to kill.

"If you're thinking of killing me, come to my head office, although it is quite a fair distance away from Edalbire and I really don't think you can afford to leave the country right now."

"You-"

"Ah, watch your language, you're forgetting, i'm your boss, I ain't gonna take any insults you throw my way sitting down."

"Fuck you!"

"Good, good, let the hate flow through you and channel it to the rebellion, i'm sure you can kill their leader."

"However that does present us with a little teensy winsey, tiny, timey-wimey problem."

"Huh?"

"Just how do you intend to get the leader into this room incase plan A fails?"

He just remains silent.

"You don't have a back-up plan do you?"

No response from him.

"Why am I not surprised?"

"Anyway, we need to talk about a possible plan B and C."

"You know they're not weak right?"

"Yes, hell some of their members are undercover CF members."

Hearing that knocks him off guard.

"I'm sorry, what?"

"Oh yeah, you didn't know? Some of the members of the Blood Renegades are spies sent in by TCF."

"But that doesn't make sense, don't they kill spies?"

"Yes but I really don't think their leader has figured it out yet, I mean everyone in the rebellion did grow up in Edalbire and all have the same goal so it's only natural to assume that members of your group aren't spies if you're that exclusive."

"I guess."

"However they would be smart to weed them out soon, I have it on good authority that the those members are ordered to do some stuff they probably don't want to do as soon as they start the raid."

"Ok? Why are you telling me this?"

"Simple, i'm making life easier for you."

"And how exactly will this make things easier for me?"

Audible facepalming can be heard coming from the monitor.

"Are you really that thick? Did I employ the wrong sibling to rule over Edalbire?"

"Would your sister have been a better candidate?"

Suddenly, his face turns to rage rather then annoyance.

"Or how about your beloved papa? Mother? Uncle? Oh fun fact: I hear that your uncle is even due to appear on the news tonight."

"DON'T YOU DARE MENTION THEM!!!"

"Hit a nerve did I?"

"I'll never forgive you for what you made me do!"

"Oh come on, now who was it that said he'd do anything to make sure he gets the throne?"

No response comes from him.

"You know, I distinctly remember it being someone who looked alot like you, well, exactly like you to be perfectly honest."

"SHUT UP!"

"Hey, i'm only stating the facts, you didn't have to do what you did, that was of your own free will."

Not having any retort to that, he punches the monitor.

"Oh wow, if I was actually there, that probably would have done some major damages."

"LEAVE ME THE FUCK ALONE DAMNIT."

"Oh and what about those innocent people you killed with your sword?"

"I heard that recently, they came back in a nightmare you had."

"SHUT UP, SHUT UP, SHUT UP, SHUT UP, SHUT UP!!!!!"

"Fine, i've gotta go anyway."

The monitor turns off and not surprisingly, he starts punching the wall in a fit of rage.

FLASHBACK: 2018

A 17 year old Prince Kingston is standing in the castle throne room, wearing royal garments like those often seen in fairy tales with rather tidy hair and standing up straight.

Meanwhile his sister: 17 year old Princess Kingston is standing next to him, she however has long blonde hair, a bright pink dress and white gloves.

The two are stood in the presence of the King and Queen of Edalbire: Oscar and Charlotte Kingston.

They both have outfits that look like they've just come out of a fairy tale with a king and queen as well.

Oscar starts talking, who is then followed by Charolette

"Kids, we know that soon, we're going to have to give up the throne and pass it onto the next generation."

"Yep and for that, we have a request for you both."

The Princess starts speaking

"What's that mother?"

"We want you two to rule together, much like us two."

"Wait, you serious father?"

"Yes, I am, 100% serious."

The Princess squeals up and down with joy.

"Hear that Sethy, we're gonna rule together, We can make Edalbire an even better paradise then it already is now."

Hearing that come from their daughter put a wholesome smile on Oscar and Charlotte's faces.

The Princess hugs both her parents then Seth himself, however while Oscar and Charlotte return the hugs, Seth doesn't, instead he just stands there.

"Sethy? What's wrong?"

"It's nothing, I just need some time alone to prepare and get my mind round it."

"We understand son, take as long as you need."

With that, Seth leaves the room and the princess starts to follow him but is stopped by Charlotte.

"Dear, we know you care about your brother but he probably just needs some time alone right now, i'm sure he'll be back to his usual chirpy self soon."

The princess then looks to her parents with happiness.

"Okie doke."

She then leaves the room, leaving Oscar and Charlotte on their own.

"Oscar, are we sure about this? They do fight."

"Yeah, plus every sibling their age fights, it's only natural, what'd be concerning is if they get along rather peachly."

"Yeah, I guess, I just worry about them, you know?"

"Yeah, so do I but they're both nearly adults, they're gonna be taking over when they hit 20 in three years."

"True, at least it gives us plenty of time to prepare their inaugurations."

"Yep."

They continue chatting, however this time about other things.

Meanwhile, in Seth's room which looks identical to his room in the present.

"Fuck, fuck, fuck, fuck, fuck, fuck, fuck, fuck!"

In the middle of all those fucks, a monitor flies in through his window and on the screen is a silhouette of a person.

"Am I in the presence of Seth Kingston?"

He turns around to see the where the noise came from, only to find the monitor.

"Wha- who are you?"

"Who I am is of no importance right this stage buf if you really must know...they call me Purge."

Hearing that causes Seth to jump back onto his bed, he had heard of Purge and no good things.

"Why are you here?"

"It's simple, I wanna make a deal with you Seth."

"What sort of deal...?"

"Right, well, you wanna rule this sorry excuse for a country right?"

"Yeah."

"So, how about you murder your parents?"

Yet again, that causes Seth to jump back in disbelief, he can't believe what he's hearing.

"Now, now, hear me out cause I believe that this can be a win/win situation for us both."

"...I'm listening."

"Well, you know how you don't want to rule with your sister?"

"Yes...? Plus how do you know that?"

"I could tell through your facial expression when your parents announced it."

"Wha- how did you-?"

"They should really up their security, it was child's play breaking into it."

"Anyways, if you kill your parents and do whatever with your sister; kill her, kick her out, let her rule with you, I personally don't care, not only will you be able to rule however YOU want to rule."

"Following on from that as well, i'll also be able to provide my own soliders to work for you and i'll make sure they obey your every command."

"But, won't that make you more vulnerable?"

"You'd think so but security is pretty tight here."

"Also, how is it a win for you?"

Seth has a confused look on his face, despite that though, the look in his eyes are saying that he's actually considering this.

"That's not for you to worry about at this moment, i'll give you more info on that later."

"Anyways, it's entirely up to you on weather or not to do it, remember you don't have to and you can just forget that we ever had this conversation."

The monitor leaves the room via the window and Seth goes deep into thought.

'Do I really want to...? Do I really want to kill my parents just to rule the country on my own?'

A few hours later, he's interrupted by the knock of someone, that someone being his sister.

"Come in."

The Princess walks in.

"Sethy? You ok?"

"Oh, sis, yeah I am, listen, I apologise for what I how I acted before, I just wanted some time alone."

"I understand, I'm sorry if I invaded your personal space."

"Nono, it's quite alright sis, listen, I never hugged you back when you hugged me earlier, so, wanna hug now?"

Her eyes light up and she rushes over to Seth who hugs her.

A few minutes later, they part from the hug and the princess starts to leave the room.

"Sis, wait, just want you to know that, whatever happens, we'll always stick by each other...promise?"

"Promise."

And with that, she closes the door as she leaves the room.

Another few hours later; it's pitch black outside, Seth's room light is on as he looks at his clock...it's fast approaching midnight, he looks at his sword which is attached to his waist and leaves his room.

He goes down the hallway, finding his parent's room, he puts an ear to the door and confirms that they're asleep.

Before doing the deed, he looks at his sword again and is starting to have second thoughts.

'Am I really going to do this? Wouldn't I just be happier ruling with my sister? What would happen if the truth gets out?'

Eventually he swallows, unsheaths his sword and slowly opens the door, as to not wake up Oscar and Charlotte.

He makes sure that the door is closed as so his sister doesn't peek in and accidentally notice what's going on.

'Sis is too pure and wholesome...damnit...do I really wanna do this to her...?'

After a few minutes of thoughts similar to those, he manages to get his head clear of them and approaches the bed.

He takes one last look at his parents before....

Blood goes all over the bed and on the sword, Oscar died straight away, however Charlotte has a little bit of life left in her, with her dying face, she looks at Seth straight in the eyes, who just looks emotionless now.

"Why Seth....why?"

Instead of answering that however, he stabs her with the sword once more thus killing her.

A few seconds later, he comes to and realises what he's done and as such, starts crying.

His sister hears the commotion and opens the door slightly to check what's going on and that's when it happens...that's when she screams really loudly.

That scream not only alerts Seth but also the nearby guards who come rushing to the area only to see Seth with his hands on the sword that just killed his parents.

Instead of saying anything however, he manages to dry his eyes and go back into an emotionless state, which leads him to be able to kill every guard that comes his way mercilessly.

While he's killing those guards left, right and centre, all his sister can do is just watch on in horror, eventually, he's able to overpower them and points his sword at her heart.

After the guards are dead, there's a whole bunch of blood splatter on the walls and floors of both the bedroom and hallway.

He goes in for the stab, only to stop at the last second and instead re-sheaths his sword, despite the blood still on it.

The princess is unable to say anything right now, not because she's being forced to stay quiet but because she has no idea how to process what just happened.

"Come with me."

She follows him to the throne room.

"W...w...what happened, S...s...Sethy..."

They arrive in the room.

"Remember our promise?"

"You mean to always stick by each other?"

"Yeah that one, well after seeing what just happened, do you realy want to still stick by me? I understand if you don't."

"W...w...will you kill me if I don't?"

"No, I could never harm you sis."

"..."

"No, I won't, I don't want to stick by a remorseless murderer!"

"I see, I respect that choice."

Seth presses a button which opens the floor where the Princess is standing, as such, she falls down the slide that's present and eventually lands in the mud outside, making her dress and hair all dirty.

Before running away, she takes one last look at the castle.

"Why Sethy...why?"

After saying that to herself, she starts to run away, where to? She doesn't know, she just keeps running and running and running until eventually, she's unable to take anymore and collapses on the pavement.

An unknown amount of time later, she wakes up and next to her is a girl around the same age with red and blue messy hair, a gothic top, a red bow tie, biker jeans and gothic boots.

The princess looks down and notices that she's not wearing her usual dress, instead she's got jeans on as well as a jean jacket and a plain white top on under that.

"Wha- Where am I? Who are you?"

"Firstly, you're in the hospital and secondly, well...everyone just calls me gothboy."

Gothboy looks at the princess with a wholesome smile.

"Hosptial?"

"Yep, you're lucky I found you the other day, which reminds me, you're the princess right?"

Instead of saying anything, she sits up, looks down. Sadly.

"I see, may I ask why you're down here with us common folk?"

Yet again, no response.

"Ah, can't really blame ya for being secretive, especially to someone you just met."

"How long was I out for?"

Gothboy turns to look at her computer.

"Judging by this, around 3-4 days."

"Did I miss anything?"

"A few things, the two big ones were the sad announcement of Oscar and Charlotte's death by Seth and that he was going to take over as king, effective immediately."

"I see..."

"Well, a few things have slightly changed since he took over, but I don't really see anything changing drastically anytime soon."

Flash forward: 2025

Seth is still in the throne room, punching his wall, soon after, he is able to regain his composure and looks outside the window: Pitch black night, at that point, he looks at the clock: 20:00.

All the robots start entering the throne room one by one, thankfully it was big enough to house so many robots.

After a few minutes, every single robot that had been made up to that point, which was too many to count, had somehow managed to all fit in the throne room while also giving Seth room to walk around to talk about his plan.

"I don't know what time, however at some point between midnight tonight and midnight the next day, the rebels are going to be storming this castle so I want every single of you defending each floor and the general outside entrance area of the castle."

"HOWEVER..."

He shows a picture of Hockface/the leader of the rebellion and explains in detail what to do, should any end up in combat with them.

Every robot speaks at once.

"SIR, YES SIR!"

"Wonderful."

He looks down at his watch: 22:00

'Wow, was I really explaining for that long?'

"Anyway, all of you charge up, I am going to need you all at 100%"

As the robots leave the room, Seth turns on the TV and on it, is the same interview that the rebellion are watching, he just keeps on watching until the half 11 broadcast, at which point he notices all the monitors on the buildings in Tehctar light up with the logo of the rebellion.

'Shit, they actually are planning something, but what?'

He keeps watching while the reporter talks to Seth's uncle.

"Yeah right old man, like me and her are ever gonna make up...I knew I should have killed her and you when I had the chance."

"Reminicing are we?"

Purge's monitor appears out nowhere, however, much like before, it's only her silhouette that appears on it.

"What do you want?"

"I don't wanna miss this, when else am I gonna get the opportunity to witness a rebellion's plans actually take effect first hand?"

"You mean the other countries you've taken don't have stuff like this?"

"Well they do but their leaders actually know how to deal with rebellions."

"Just shut up, you're really getting on my nerves."

"Oh gee and I thought I was in your good books."

"HA, In your dreams."

"Bold of you to assume that I actually have dreams."

"Oh would you shut up, i'm trying to watch this."

"Ohhhh, fussypants, fine."

The two look to the TV and just continue watching the broadcast.

"This is boring, is there anything else on?"

Instead of responding, Seth just ignores Purge and continues watching.

Soon, 23:55 rolls around.

"This just in, the screens all have a 5 minute countdown on them and with it being 11:55PM, i'm guessing that they're waiting until midnight to deliver their message and with only 5 minutes left, who knows what they have to say...stay tuned."

"Oh no, I just hope that nothing bad comes of this and that we can be one happy family again."

"By the way Mr. Kingston, do you happen to know just how Oscar and Charolette died?"

"Yes I do because I saw the aftermath with my own eyes."

"Would you be willing to explain to our viewers?"

"Can it wait until after the rebellion's message?"

"Of course."

After a few minutes of idle chatting bewteen Mr. Kingston and the reporter, midnight rolls around and the video message that Gothboy made starts playing:

Firstly Hockface speaks

"Greetings people of Edalbire, no doubt you've heard of us, but for those uninitiated, we are the Blood Renegades, rebels as some people like to call us and well, we come to you all tonight with a simple message."

Gasmask follows:

"His Royal Highness; Seth Kingston not only usurped the throne from the rightful heir but also did some dirty things to get into that position in the first place."

Next, Stopwatch:

"So because of that, good people of Edalbire, our message is this: Cause as much chaos as you can and help us tonight to force Seth of the throne and put the rightful princess back on."

Gothboy:

"With everyone's help, we can bring the country back to it's peaceful self."

The rest of the silhouettes of the rebels:

"Good luck Edalbire."

The message stops and the news broadcast comes back.

"Ok then...that was uhh...interesting..."

Some glass shattering happens behind the reporter.

"What the- Ok, viewers, i'm going to try and keep this broadcast running for as long as I can, however if I join everyone, i'm taking the cameras with me so you can get first hand footage."

Outside the castle windows, Seth can see fires happening as well as hearing gunshots being fired, however he doesn't know if it's a rebellion member who fired the guns or people protesting/rioting who managed to get their hand on one.

Him, Hockface and very likely many of the citizens all knew that Edalbire was basically teetering on the edge, just waiting for someone to push it over and while it took a bit longer then many had thought; the rebellion had finally done it.

He looks down at the crumbling city of Tehctar, no law, no order, just absolute chaos with rubble flying everywhere, buildings on fire, people shouting all over, gunshots being fired and glass being shattered.

If the Blood Renegades threats were true then both him and Hockface know that today is...judgement day.

'I've been waiting for this day for so long Hockface.'

He goes to his throne, grabs his sword which is sitting next to it and sheaths it, seemingly preparing for a fight, most likely with Hockface.

Seth knows that in less then 24 hours, either him or Hockface will be dead in their final showdown.

Judgement Day: 00:00-06:00

A few minutes past midnight, in the rebel briefing room, every rebel is there waiting for orders from the team leaders, despite that though, they're the only ones there, the leaders aren't anywhere to be seen and as such, there's idle chatter going on between the rebellion.

Outside the fires can be smelt from inside the briefing room, causing some rebels to cover their noses, along with those, the sound of constant glass shattering all over the place is heard, with some bits of debris even hitting the windows of the base.

Along with those, really loud cars are heard speeding past as well as sirens from all three emergency services, even if one of them is in Seth's pocket, there's no two ways around it, Edalbire is in full chaos.

"Did you see that broadcast a few minutes ago?"

"Shit, Alot of us are gonna be dead."

"I know but it'll be worth it for those who survive, haven't you ever seen any rebellion stories?"

"Yeah, the rebellion always wins, but this isn't a story, this is real life."

"Ok, i'll give you that one."

More idle chatter like that keeps happening until the leaders:

Hockface

Gothboy

Gasmask

And

Vetry

All walk into the room together, Once they are there, everyone shuts up to let them speak.

Hockface starts speaking firstly.

"Right, listen up, no doubt by now that you've all seen the broadcast that we made, well tonight we strike at the heart of all this."

"As per usual, you are going to be split up into different teams, I will be leading the flanking team, Gothboy here will be leading the front strike team, Gasmask will be leading the assassination team and Vetry will be leading the strategy team."

"For those in my team, we are going to be going round the back of the castle and raiding from there, there should be an entrance around the back, however The King is smart, so it'll very likely be heavily guarded."

"Once we find the entrance, we first make our way to where he kept Science Lab and rescue him, after which, we'll make our way to the throne room for the final showdown, any questions?"

A random rebel puts their hand up.

"Yeah, one: Where's Proto?"

"That, i'm not sure about, however it's probably best that it's in hiding right now, anymore questions?"

No more questions for the time being.

"Right, who's going next?"

Gothboy steps forwards.

"We're going to be storming in straight through the front and killing any robots we see along the way, much like the back, we also expect the front of the castle to be heavily guarded, once we're inside however, we will be rendezvousing with the Flank team."

"Any questions?"

No questions.

"Okie dokey, who's next?"

Gasmask steps forwards.

"Right, our team will be split into four:

Group A will be with the flank team

Group B will be with the front strike team

Group C will be taking the left side of the castle with me

And

Group D will be taking the right side of the castle, however, as the name implies, you need to assassinate any enemies that the other teams miss or in the case of C and D, we'll be sticking in the shadows and assassinating the enemies."

"Once inside the castle, rather then joining up with Flank and Front strike, we're instead tasked with looking for prisoners and freeing them, killing any guards we see along the way."

"Any questions?"

No rebel has any questions.

Finally, Vetry steps forwards.

"Our team will be the strategists, we will be providing live updates to the other teams on the whereabouts of where each guard is should they move or if any should sneak behind them."

"To keep tabs on the whole situation, we've got four of these."

Four drones all fly into the room.

"These will give us live 360 degree footage of all the events unfolding at the castle, both inside and out."

"We will be controlling them from a secret location that the guards won't know about because if they spot them then there's a 100% chance that they'll be led back to here and blow the place up in the process so make sure that if you have anything here, you take it with you because we will not be coming back."

All rebels nod after hearing that and Hockface speaks next.

"Right, anyone have any questions?"

No one speaks.

"Perfect, go with your assigned teams and they'll tell you what to do from there."

As if in sync, every rebel speaks at once.

"Roger, Roger."

The teams all leave the room, however while they're walking out, helicopters can be heard flying by, Seth didn't have any helicopters, he's got no reason for them what with his robots so out of curiosity everyone looks outside.

Once outside, everyone notices that the riots managed to attract the attention of international news outlets who are no doubt reporting it live for their viewers back home.

While looking at the helicopters, each rebel can also smell fires happening all over, and even see the ones that are on the road they're currently on, thanks to all this rioting and chaos, the sky has also turned a very dark shade of red.

After looking at everything for a minute, the rebels, with the exception of Hockface's team, all head back inside.

Her team arrives at the garage and once there, she starts going over the plan.

"Right, i'm only gonna say this once, ok?"

"YES MA'AM!"

"We split up into two and go around opposite sides to the back of the castle, because if we don't, a certain someone will most likely be able to take all of us out in one go, however if we split up, he's going to have to choose which side to attempt to take out."

"Ma'am, question."

"Yes?"

"Which side are you going?"

"Left."

"Gotcha."

"Once we all meet up at the back of the castle and have decommissioned each robot round there, that's when we go on, once in, the rest of you will rendezvous with Gasmask's team in an attempt to rescue as many people as possible."

"What about you? And Gothboy's team?"

"Me: i'm making a beeline for the throne room and I know what you're gonna ask, while I do appreciate the help, this is going to be something I need to do on my own and in regards to Gothboy's team: they're sticking on robot killing duty."

"Gotcha."

"So, what'll happen at the end?"

"The rightful heir will be on the throne and peace will return to Edalbire."

"..."

"Anymore questions?"

"How long is this going to take?"

"If everything works out perfectly: 23 hours, if not then well...we may be going into multiple days."

"Alrighty."

Hockface doesn't speak for ten seconds to allow other rebels to get any questions they want in, however no-one speaks up and as such, she continues talking.

"Righty-o, oh also one last thing, if any of you find Science Lab, bring him back safely."

"Roger, roger."

When Hockface finishes speaking, all the rebels on her team, each go into cars, filling them up, once everyone is in, she starts speaking on the walkie-talkie.

"To make this easier, everyone on my side will be taking the left route and everyone on the other side will be taking the right route, just so we don't get confused, we'll go first then you'll follow behind."

"We'll meet you at the back of the castle, or you'll meet us there, anyways, let's get going."

The left side cars all leave the garage who are followed by the right side ones a few seconds after the final left side car leaves.

Meanwhile, back in the living room of the rebel base, Gothboy is talking with her team.

"Uhhh, question: How would we storm the front of the castle without the cars."

"Easy, follow me."

The teams all follow Gothboy.

"While we're walking there, anyone got any questions, or conversation topics to pass the time?"

"I do have one actually, where are we going?"

"Outskirts of Tehctar, I'm going to show you all the little toy we'll be playing with during our side of the raid."

Each of these rebels knew Gothboy and when she said 'little toy', they knew it was going to be something big, however big though is going to remain a mystery until they get there.

"When will our team strike the castle?"

"Literally as soon as we get on this toy, that's when we set off."

After a little more walking, they finally get to an airfield where once they open up one of the garages inside it, are a bunch of vehicles, including the quadbike Science Lab was working on a while back, however the main attraction is one giant tank that looks larger then any normal tank.

All the rebels walk up to the tank and look up in awe as they get closer to it.

"This is our little toy."

Feeling a wave of disbelief, each rebel climbs onto the tank, however they notice that the bits above the treds are big enough to house humans in and as such, each one sits there.

"Gothboy, question: How the hell did you get this beast?"

"Some buddies of mine owed me a favour."

Once each Rebel is in and armed, Gothboy climbs into the driver's seat of the tank, starts the engine and get's it moving.

"Oh great thing about this thing: It can withstand a whole slew of explosions, as long as you're inside those compartments, unless we get hit by either 20 rockets at once OR a nucluear bomb, we should be golden."

While Gothboy is driving that tank, back at the rebel base, Gasmask and her team are all sitting on the floor with a giant sheet of paper, currently visualising and planning their attack.

"Before we continue, I do have one question: How are we going to get to the castle, it's on the otherside of the city."

Vetry comes downstairs and overhears that.

"I don't know if you guys are aware but just on the outskirts of the city, there's-"

Before Vetry can finish talking, they all hear a heavy engine as well as feel rumbling on the ground, so like before with the helicopters, they go outside to check.

Once they're outside, they see Gothboy's team on a giant tank, cheering and being chaotic, while watching, Gothboy ends up driving over and crushing a small green and black car that in the eyes of the people in the tank, looked rather Mini.

"Did that car look familiar to anyone?"

Everyone looks to that rebel and shakes their head, once the tank has been crushed, a man in a brown jacket, red tie, black trousers and white shirt comes by and is visibly pissed, despite that though, he just mutters unintelligably.

Once that has passed, Gasmask's team go back inside to continue the visualisation and Vetry tries to speak again.

"As I was saying, I don't know if you guys are aware but on the outskirts of the city, there is an airfield where we keep a bunch of our vehicles that Science Lab worked on before his well...unfortunate kidnapping."

One of the rebels looks to Vetry.

"Yeah, but don't you need like some sorta special access key or something to access it?"

"Initally yes, however from the strategy room, I can override that and well, I did just that for this occasion so when you're done planning, you should just be able to waltz right in, if you can't just let me know and i'll fix it for ya."

And with that, Vetry walks back upstairs.

"So guys, now that, that's out of the way and we have our routes, should we get going?"

The rebels agree, all of them get up and leave the base to start walking to the airfield, after around 20 minutes of walking, they arrive at the airfield where the doors were already open and so, they were able to see inside the garages.

Once in, they each inspect the vehicles on offer, opting for for a helicopter, once in, due to none of them knowing how to pilot one, Gasmask enters the locations of the drop off points for each team and they start flying.

"Damn, Tehctar looks weirdly scenic right now, despite being in flames."

"Yes, but remember, we're not here to take in the views, anyway, if you stop for just a few minutes down there, you're dead."

The helicopter continues flying over Tehctar, going past not only the vehicles from the other teams but also a few news helicopters with one even managing to catch up to the Gasmask's team.

Once the helicopter is close enough, the door on the news one opens and Gasmask gives the go ahead for a the door near the news one to open.

Once it's open, both the reporter and rebels have to shout due to the noises from the helicopters.

"Thanks for agreeing to this interview, I only have a few questions!"

"It will only take five minutes!"

"Can it wait until after we're done?"

"Question 1: Can you tell our viewers at home, just exactly what this revolution is about?"

Gasmask starts talking now.

"Look reporter, i'm sure you're a professional at your job but we can't do an interview until later, if you want though, you are more then welcome to follow us if you can keep up."

And with that, the doors on both helicopters close with the rebels one going further ahead to one side of the castle, the doors on their helicopter opens and a bunch of rebels jump onto a pipe and make their way down.

Once those rebels are out, the helicopter goes to the other side and the exact same thing happens and as soon as all those are out, it goes to the back and Gasmask's team drops down, however they need use their parachutes to get down safely due to the lack of any sewage pipes around the back.

Meanwhile, the rebels on both sides of the castle, can see the tank that Gothboy's team is on closing in, they know that soon, the rockets from the tank are going to hit inside the castle rather soon-ish, meanwhile around the sides, Hockface's teams start to show up, while Gasmask's are just breaking in, once noticing, both sides, offer to help them in via the window they were able to sneak into.

However round the back, Hockface herself and her side are no-where to be seen, despite that their cars are already there, so once noticing that, Gasmask's team comes to the conclusion that they must already be inside.

And lo and behold, they were correct, once inside, Gasmask's team catches up with the front rebel team and soon after, both side teams join up.

"Right guys, question: Where's Hockface?"

One of her team speaks up after Gasmask asks that.

"Not sure, all we were told was that there was something she had to do on her own, but what? No clue and we don't know where she is either."

"I see, does anyone know what the time is?"

Gasmask looks at her watch:

"We are 6 hours into this operation, we now need to wait for Vetry's locations and Gothboy's signals."

Judgement Day 06:00-12:00

In the throne room, Seth is looking outside the window, seeing his robots fighting rebels from the front, completely unaware that there's already quite a few rebels inside the castle, while watching however, one of the robots comes into the throne room.

"SIR, WE REGRET TO INFORM YOU THAT A TON OF REBELS HAVE MADE INSIDE THE CASTLE!"

He turns around, clearly enraged after hearing that.

"WHAT!?!?!? DIDN'T I ORDER YOU TO KILL ANY REBELS YOU SEE!??!!?"

"YES YOU DID, HOWEVER WE DID NOT KNOW THAT THEY CAME IN UNTIL WE CHECKED THE SECURITY SYSTEM."

"ARE YOU FUCKING KIDDING ME!?!?! YOU WERE SUPPOSED TO BE STAIONED OUTSIDE ANY POSSIBLE AREAS WHERE THEY COULD BREAK IN, THE ONLY ONES ACTUALLY TRYING TO TAKE OUT THE REBELLION ARE THE ONES AT THE FRONT!!!"

"YES SIR!"

He takes a few deep breaths to calm down, after which, he shows a picture of Hockface.

"Find the rebels and kill them, if you see this one however, bring them to me."

"UNDERSTOOD SIR"

The robot leaves the throne room and Seth starts thinking to himself as the sun starts rising.

He looks to the ground outside and he can see both corpses of dead rebels and broken parts of robots, he knew that there would be dead soldiers on his side.

'Just you wait Blood Renegades, tonight, you all will...DIE!"

Meanwhile back in the hallway, the rebels that broke in are currently planning.

"Right, seeing as we're basically one team now, should we split into two or three groups."

Gasmask responds.

"I'd say three groups, it allows us to cover more ground."

"Roger, roger"

The rebels start to split up into three groups, however before they can, from all directions, they're greeted by waves of Seth's robots running down with some having a gun in place of an hand and others having swords.

Left right and centre, the sounds of steel swords going through skin, gunshots making contact with both metal and flesh, metal falling on the floor from the robots that are destroyed and the bodies of rebels that are killed during this fight.

Soon after, they are able to thin out the robot's ranks and the ones who are still alive, keep to the split up plan after very quickly paying their respects to their fallen comrades.

Meanwhile back in the strategy room, Vetry is assissting the others and talking to Gothboy's team via a wireless communicator.

"You lot, listen to us and listen very carefully, Any second now, there's going to be robots coming at you from all sides, you WILL need to think of a plan to be able to get out of this."

"Gotcha, Vetty."

"..."

Stopwatch speaks via the communicator.

"I can be of vital help here, when I was a guard I saw these robots starting to be made and a potential weak spot, I can hack into them from here to expose it but you are only going to have one chance to destroy them."

"Stopwatch, can they be destroyed by splash damage?"

"No, somehow that shit for brains managed to make them completely splash proof."

"...Purge."

"...oh no...oh no....oh no oh no, this is bad, this is like, really, really, really bad."

The rebels in the strategy room look confusingly at Stopwatch.

Before explaining, Stopwatch manages to hack into the robots and expose their weak spots, after which, he mutes his microphone which leads to a conversation between Stopwatch and Vetry.

"You've all heard of this person who comes to people in the running for country leaders right?"

"You mean the one who goes to those who have no chance of suddenly getting in power then all of a sudden, those people are in power?"

"Yeah, if Gothboy is right and Purge is involved, Edalbire is more fucked then it may seem."

"How so?"

Stopwatch sighs.

Instead of saying anything, Stopwatch pulls up live footage of a few countries:

United Kingdom

Japan

The USA

Russia

Finland

Jamaica

And

Noilegnave

Each one of those countries have one thing in common: They all have massive riots and chaos ensuing in each of their major urban areas.

"These are just a few of the countries that had their current leaders in situations like what I mentioned before, but suddenly became a leader out of nowhere."

"Then within the first few months of said leaders becoming leaders, their countries found themselves in chaos much like the one we're currently in now."

"Damn..."

After that explanation, they look back at the live footage of the raid on the castle and see that all the robots that were attacking them have all been destroyed, however during that fight, there were also a few casualties.

Among the casualties, one of them is Gothboy, leaning out of the driver's seat, completely lifeless and her eyes opened, despite that though, they aren't moving at all or showing any signs of life.

One of the few alive rebels on the team speaks via communicator.

"Guys...We won that fight but at a cost...the leader of our team: Gothboy...is dead."

Vetry's voice suddenly goes very shaky and they shout into the microphone.

"N...N....N...NO, THAT CAN'T BE TRUE...SURELY SHE'S STILL ALIVE....NO, SHE CAN'T BE DEAD!!!!"

"I'm sorry Vetry, I really am but she is unfortunately dead, I checked all over for a pulse but there aren't any that I can find."

After hearing that, Vetry just drops to the ground on their knees and are trying really hard not to cry right now, however that's failing as their are tears currently streaming down their face right now.

The rebels help Vetry to the couch, some stay to comfort them, others go back to the strategy table, including Stopwatch who puts the microphone on.

"While Vetry is out of commission, does everyone mind if I take over as leader?"

No one has any objections to that, once that is revealed, Stopwatch unmutes his microphone.

"Ok guys, while Vetry is out of commission, i'm going to take over as the strategy team leader."

The few currently alive members of Gothboy's team agree to that.

"Right, so with only a few of you left, it's probably best if you forgo your original plan and stick together, the other two teams should be somewhere in the castle, although while I don't know exactly where, I do have a rough idea."

"They should be somewhere near the prison cells, that's if he's not executed them yet, I do know how to get to the cells from there but because I can't see inside, I can only say the directions once, ok?"

"Gotcha."

"Keep straight until you hit the giant hall then turn right, enter that door infront of you, once done, turn left then left again, finally turn right and keep straight then the cells will be on your right."

"If there's no-one in the cells then they may be in the dungeon which is just down the stairs at the end of prison room, if not then...unless another team beat you to it, i'm afraid that by that point, they're executed."

Each perons nods and they start running.

Stopwatch turns off the live stream and goes back to Vetry.

Meanwhile, back in the castle, the few members of Gothboy's team are running until they hit the giant hall that Stopwatch mentioned.

Some of them started to go through the hall to the door, however another one stops them.

"Wait...something smells fishy here..."

"Agreed, this feels too easy."

"Yeah...not that, I mean something literally smells."

The other four stop and sniff, they smell something as well.

"What is it?"

The one who found out about the smell follows their nose to a vent.

"Hey guys, the smell's coming from here, could someone give me a leg up?"

All of them go over, however only one helps lift up the other.

Once they eventually manage to get the vent open, rats come running out of it, causing them to fall down and rub their heads in pain.

"Ow, everyone ok?"

They check on two of the rebels that have their eyes closed, however those two are only uncouncious, most likely from the sudden thud of their heads hitting the ground.

"So, did you see anything in there?"

"Didn't get a chance to thanks to those rats, you'd think a castle like this would be kept in tip top wouldn't you?"

"Yeah."

"Anyways, could you give me a leg up again?"

"Sure."

The two do the same, however once the rebel gets a proper look inside, they look all around until eventually seeing something that they didn't want to see, not in a million years.

"Find anything?"

The rebel on the ground after asking that can feel them shaking and are able to hear them stifling a scream.

Still trying to make sense of what's in his front of him though, he tries touching the corpse to see if there's any movement, however there isn't any, no signs of life either.

"Dude, you ok? What's up there?"

However after a minute or so of panicking and trying to take deep breaths, that rebel finally lets out a really loud scream that can be heard all over the vents and by extension, all over the castle.

"Shit, what's up there dude?"

The rebel crouches then jumps down onto the ground.

"No, just...."

Before they can even finish, they're panicking like crazy.

"Dude, deep breaths, take deep breaths and count to ten."

That rebel does that multiple times and are eventually able to calm down.

"So, should we get going once those two wake up?"

Instead of saying anything, that rebel just nods and the three currently awake just sit on a really long table.

"Hey, you two, seeing as today might be our final day alive, what's one thing you regret not doing when you had the chance to?"

Before any could speak, the two start to wake up and the three check on them, to make sure that they can still move.

Once confirmed that they can, they make their way back to the door they were meant to go through and continue on with their mission.

Eventually, they reach the prison cells where there's a few cells unopened, although they have no-one in them, the rest of the cells are open and empy, so remembering what Stopwatch said, the five go down into the dungeon to see if there's anyone there.

Once down there, they find there's a few people, some prisoners who were being prepped for execution and some rebels trying to free them.

Instead of saying anything and trying to make conversation, the five rebels who just entered the room help get the prisoners free and all of them escort them outside via the side entrance.

One of the rebels hands a slip of paper over.

"Guys, go to this address, there's someone there who can get you in a secret tunnel to start a new life and make sure not to get caught on the way there."

Once those people have gone, a rebel that was already in the room stops Gothboy's team.

"Hey, what's going on? Where's Gasmask and Gothboy?"

"A: Helping you and B:..."

They knew they had to mention this sooner or later.

"...Gasmask and Gothboy are both dead."

Hearing that sends the rebels into a shock, they weren't expecting to hear that, the team leaders are very quickly being picked off one by one, but by who? Surely it can't just be any robot right?

After that conversation, the rebels go to the front of the castle and while the tank is still there, Gothboy herself is still missing.

"No...they couldn't have got rid of the body already could they?"

"Don't know but these robots do act quick if they have, how long ago did you find her body over the driver's seat?"

"Three hours ago."

"I see, so you found it at around 7 right?"

"Yep, what's with all the questions? It's like i'm being interrogated by the police or something."

"Sorry, force of habit."

"It's ok, I just hope Vetry, Stopwatch and Hockface are ok."

"Same, so what now? Our mission is done, the others inside are still doing theirs however."

"Should we go and help them?"

"Maybe but we have no idea where they are and what if we accidentally bump into one of the robots completely unprepared."

"Yeah, good point."

"Say, do you know where Hockface went?"

"Nope."

Out of nowhere, Seth starts a live broadcast which as per usual, is shown on every TV and monitor in Edalbire.

"I knew this day would come eventually, the day that you weaklings would try to dethrone me, well i've got a fun little fact for ya: A little birdy told me that some of your team leaders are dead."

"Wha-"

"Now, I know what you're thinking...."

He tries and fails to put on a child sounding voice to mock the Blood Renegades, that shows just how he truly sees them: Not as formidable foes but instead as little kids.

"But how can they die, we're so strong and invicible and stuff."

His voice is back to normal.

"Well, to answer that question, my robots were able to overpower them, simple as, no two ways round it, no fancy gimmicks or anything like that, just the robots killing them...ok, I suppose the robot COULD count as a fancy gimmick but these models are in mass production, anyone can have one."

"So there's just one thing i'd like to leave you all with for now..."

"You childish Blood Renegades will die....TONIGHT!!!!!"

And with that, the broadcast shuts off.

After that broadcast shuts off, only a few of the rebels that were inside go out and see Gothboy's team, just standing in the courtyard, in a field of broken robots and bloodied corpses.

With Hockface's whereabouts unknown, Gasmask, Gothboy and around 90% of the rebellion dead, the chances of them even winning this thing are next to 0%.

At this point, their only hope now is to basically work together as one team instead of many separate teams and take down any robots they see coming, while starting to make their way to the throne room.

Breaking the ice, one of the rebels from Gothboy's side starts speaking

"So...let me guess...everyone who was with you is dead?"

One of the rebels who came out of the castle sigh and instead of saying anything, just nod.

"There is a small plus however: The innocents we rescued are currently on their way to The Netherlands as we speak."

"That's amazing, hey I have an idea: How about we get the rioting citizens to raid the castle and find Hockface with us? If it's only us 8, we're dead, no matter what."

"It could work but do you have any idea how you'll get their attention?"

One of the rebels looks to the tank that Gothboy was driving.

"Hmmm..."

Instead of saying anything, they go to inspect it.

"How about we use this?"

"How so?"

"Someone takes it into the city and fires it up in the air, at which point, we say our intentions and pray to whatever deity you believe in, if you do that at least some join us."

"Honestly, we could do with as much help as we need so go right ahead."

An hour later, the 7 other rebels are waiting by the castle, they've not heard anything from Hockface or Vetry in a while and as such, are now starting to really worry about them both.

"You think Vetry's all right?"

"I don't know, I just hope those robots didn't break in."

Meanwhile, back at the base, a bunch of rebels, including Vetry and Stopwatch are currently fighting off robots that managed to break in, with literally any weapon they can find.

So far, they are doing a decent job, despite being majorly outnumbered, however, that very quickly takes a turn for the worse as Stopwatch is suddenly collapsed out nowhere along with the rebels who are already dead.

Soon, most of the robots and most of the rebels in the room are dead, leaving only Vetry and one last robot.

"ONLY ONE VITAL SIGN DETECTED."

Instead of saying anything or retaliating, Vetry just puts their hand up.

"YOU ARE VETRY, CORRECT?"

"What's it to you?"

"DO YOU KNOW T.R.A.C.E?"

That name rung a bell with Vetry, they recognised it but, how did the robot know who that was, all of these were manufactured by Seth and his cronies right?

Instead of answering however, Vetry spits at the robot and puts a small capsule against their teeth.

After that happens, the robot points it's gun at Vetry.

Sounding muffled, they give the robot an ultimatum.

"Shoot me and we both die, leave and we both live, your choice."

Without thinking, the robot starts to shoot, however noticing it happen, Vetry quickly swallows the capsule and collapses to the ground.

"NO LIFE SIGNS DETECTED, WHAT DO YOU WANT ME TO DO SIR!"

"Burn the place, just to make double sure, I don't want ANYONE to be secretly alive, got that!"

"YES SIR!"

After finishing speaking to Seth, the robot starts placing explosives all over the room then all over the base.

It looks at the clock:

12:00

Hockface is missing, the team leaders are all dead and the rebellion is losing, things are looking extremely grim for the rebellion, at this point, not only do they need all the help they can get but they also need a miracle.

Will that miracle happen however? Only time will tell.

Judgement Day 12:00-18:00

An hour after being sent out in the tank, the rebel that was in the tank comes back, not only with the machine but also a bunch of supporters of the course.

"How did you- Never mind, let's go."

They jump out of the tank and walk into the castle, rather then splitting up and taking different paths, Hoping to find Hockface, no-one knows where she is...or so they thought.

Although they can't see it, A broadcast starts that they are able to hear and a voice on it sounds familiar.

"Seth Kingston, your time is up, surrender now or DIE!"

There's no mistaking it, that's Hockface, everyone there wondered however...what was she doing in the throne room in the first place?

Instead of saying anything to each other, everyone who went inside the castle goes back outside to take a look at the broadcast and lo and behold, Hockface is there, standing infront of Seth.

The two have their weapons pointed at each other: Hockface a pistol and Seth a sword.

"Oh my dear sweet Hockface, ain't that a kick in the teeth? You come all this way and just expect me to give up the throne?"

A very cocky snicker can be heard coming from Seth.

"If you want it then...."

Seth gets in a fighting pose, he's ready to strike at a moments notice.

"Then come and take it from my cold, dead hands!"

And with that, the two start duking it out, the riots in Edalbire have stopped and by extension the entire country, to watch this fight, along with those, the news helicopters broadcasting the events of today are just pointing their cameras at the various monitors all over the country.

Everyone watching knows full well just what's at stake here but only two people know truly what's completely at stake.

And that's the two fighting, to make it fair, Hockface dropped her gun and got a sword she grabbed on her way there, causing the two to fight melee instead of ranged v melee.

Seth is able to kick Hockface away causing her to fall back onto a wall.

He goes in to stab her, however she's able to get back up and deflect, thus kicking him in the balls really hard.

"OW, YOU BITCH!!!!"

Knowing that he can't afford to let them recover, the two run to each other and clash swords again, multiple times.

"You just had to persist didn't you? You couldn't just let things go on as they were!"

"No matter what, I couldn't, you killed hundreds, if not thousands of innocent people, you're not human anymore, you're just a fucking monster!"

He manages to kick her away again.

"Me, a monster? HA! That's rich coming from you."

Snarling can be heard coming from under Hockface's mask.

"No, i'm not a monster, i'm a leader!"

"Well, too bad, cause in the eyes of my subjects down there, you're the monster and i'm the hero the world needs."

"FUCKING DIEEEEEEEEEEEE!!!!!!"

The two start clashing swords again.

"Hey, look on the bright side, at least I do have just a small amount of respect for you."

"HA! Yeah right, you don't have any respect for anyone, hell you even killed your own guards, that's not respect, that's just throwing away the ruined lives of people!"

"Oh, you always were such a simple minded person, never seeing the big picture."

"Wha- What do you mean?"

"Ain't it obvious?"

"..."

Does Seth know her secret? The one Hockface wanted kept a secret at all costs? If so, how did he figure it out...or did he know all along and was just biding his time?"

While in thought, Seth takes the opportunity, to slice the mask in half but leaving the face intact...

Everyone looking at the monitors are in shock as the mask falls down, despite the blue hair, everyone instantly recognises who it is.

No-one outside of Seth and the person herself can believe their eyes, they all thought she was dead, or at least had fled the country.

But nope, she is there, alive and well.

There's no mistaking it, Hockface was Hope Kingston, Seth's very own sister, the same one he kicked out of the castle just a few years ago.

When the face was revealed, he had a completely different look to what the people of Edalbire had, much like them, he instantly recognised who Hockface really was and for a brief second, his cockiness turned to fear.

He did step back however, as it caught him off guard, he didn't know who to expect but it definitely was not his own sister.

However he was just as quickly able to regain his composure and is back to his previous cocky self.

"TAKE A GOOD LOOK AT YOUR SAVIOUR EDALBIRE!!!"

The cameras are all pointed at Hope, to say that she looks incredibly pissed off with Seth right now is an understatement.

"YOUR SAVIOUR IS NONE OTHER THEN MY SISTER, THE PRINCESS OF EDALBIRE!"

"HOW DO YOU FEEL ABOUT THAT NOW?!?!? KNOWING THAT THE ROYAL FAMILY IS INDEED ON BOTH SIDES OF THE SAME COING!!!"

"I am going to kill you..."

"What was that?"

"You're dead meat Seth Kingston."

His response is extremely sarcastic.

"Awww, this isn't what mummy and daddy deariest would want, is it?"

"YOU'RE NOT WORTHY TO MENTION THEIR NAMES!!!"

She starts lunging at him and he lunges back, the two clash their swords again.

"THEY WANTED US TO RULE TOGETHER YOU BASTARD!!!"

"NO, THEY WANTED YOU TO RULE AND ME TO JUST DO NOTHING, I COULDN'T ALLOW THAT, I JUST COULDN'T!!!"

"OH MY FUCKING GOD, YOU ARE AN IDIOT SETH KINGSTON!!!"

"YOU COMMITED HORRIBLE CRIMES AGAINST THE PEOPLE OF THIS COUNTRY, ALL FOR WHAT? YOU'RE OWN SELF GRATITUDE? DID YOU ACTUALLY THINK YOU WERE DOING A GOOD THING?!?!?!"

"Oh, Hockface, what happened to the sweet, pure, happy go lucky and could do nothing wrong girl I knew before?"

"She died when you kicked her out!"

"One word: Oof"

Hope is very visibly pissed off right now, all common sense has left her, her mind is filled with nothing but rage and murder so she lunges at him again, however while he is able to successfully block any major damage, she does scrape his arm with her sword.

That scrape does cause his shirt sleeve to rip and some blood to start coming out of his arm, however while the two are clashing swords, Seth is able to bandage his wound back up and put himself properly back into the fight.

"WHY DIDN'T YOU LISTEN TO THEM!??!?!"

"I DID, THEY JUST WANTED YOU TO RULE, YOU ALWAYS WERE THE FAVOURITE OUT OF US TWO, I WAS JUST THERE, IN MY SISTER'S SHADOW!!!"

"WELL NO MORE, I MANAGED TO STEP OUT OF YOUR SHADOW AND CARVE MY OWN LEGACY, ONE THAT WILL BE REMEMBERED FOR ALL THE RIGHT REASONS!!!"

It's too late for him, he's so delusional to the point where he genuinely thinks that he's doing good, not only for Edalbire but also the world, not even Purge could have seen this coming.

There's no turning back for him, in Hope's eyes, the only humane thing to do now is to put her brother out of his misery.

He holds out both of his arms, leaving his stomach area exposed.

"COME ON THEN!!!! IF YOU WANT TO SO BADLY, I'M RIGHT HERE!!!"

Without thinking, she goes to lunge to him but instead of going through him when the sword hits, something instead sends her flying back to the wall, also making stuff in the room a mess in the process.

In response to that, he starts giving an insane laugh.

"Really Hope? Really? I thought you were smarter then that."

While he's saying that, he's also walking to Hope with his sword in front of him, once he gets to her, he gently places the tip of it on her neck.

"Oh dear sister of mine, how things could have been very different..."

She looks into his eyes, there's no humanity left inside him, or if there is even a smidge of it, it's been locked down so far away, that even he doesn't know how to get it back.

"If only you had agreed to stay with me when I offered, we could have ruled over this wasteland, together and we could have taken it to a whole new golden age."

"Yeah, over my dead body!"

"Oh darling Hope, you're not really in a position where you can say stuff like that, you're injured."

While keeping the sword to her neck, he pulls out a rather interesting looking gun.

"Shame the rebellion wasn't stronger, I really wanted to use this, want to know what it would have done and what it's called?"

"What...?"

"It's called the Sonic Sound Wave disrupter, or the SSD for short and it basically would have temporarily disabled all your vehicles, causing so many rebels to crash into my walls, but alas, because there was much less then I anticipated, I never got to use it."

"Adding onto the fact that all your leaders are also dead, doesn't really help matters."

Hearing that causes Hope's expression to change to disbelief, was what Seth just told her true? Were all the team leaders really dead? What happened to many of the rebellion members as a whole?

"Now, I can imagine that so many questions are racing in your mind right now and rightfully so, however allow me some time to answer some of them."

"Firstly, yes, my robots did kill ALL of your team leaders and along with those, around 99% of your entire rebellion."

"I...I...I...don't believe you."

"Oh really? I do have proof of each of their deaths."

He pulls up security footage from the castle and each one shows the deaths of Gothboy, Gasmask as well as footage from the robot that burnt down the base, which also showed the death of not only Vetry swallowing their pill but also Stopwatch's already dead corpse lying on the ground.

While the footage is on, he also activates sound.

And the conversation that played before is heard, not only by Hope but also by all of Edalbire.

Once that conversation is over, he turns off the recordings.

"You know, your name is rather ironic."

"It literally means to bring light and hope but instead, you've done the opposite, you've done nothing but bring despair, not only to yourself but also your rebellion, why?"

"Because you split apart from them to chase me, that's right Hope..."

"IT'S YOUR FAULT MOST OF THE REBELLION IS DEAD!!!!"

He goes back into an insane laugh, meanwhile, Hope is just sitting against the wall speechless, was it really her fault? Was she really the reason why the rebellion was basically dead?

They could have handled themselves right? Everyone there, including the strategy team, are all trained in combat, none of them would have gone down without at least a fight...

"Oh, one last thing before I kill you, as i'm sure you've figured out but i'll say it anyway, not only are your leaders dead but along with them, around 99% of the entire rebellion is dead, infact, if you look outside this window, you can see just about every member of the rebellion that's alive."

He starts counting them.

"Eight I count, including you, that's nine."

"You bastard!"

"You lying bastard!"

"Oh? How am I a lying bastard?"

"There's no way that they're dead and..."

She is able to muster the strength to stand back up and get her sword back into position.

"Even if they are..."

She clashes her sword with Seth's.

"THE REBELLION WILL COME BACK, STRONGER THEN EVER BEFORE!!!!"

"YES, HOPE, YES, LET YOUR FAKE POSITIVITY GET YOU, IT'LL MAKE KILLING YOU EVER MORE SWEET!!!"

"THE ONLY ONE DYING HERE TONIGHT IS YOU SETH!!!"

The two start clashing swords again, however after a minute of clashing they both go behind some cover, pull out their guns and start firing at each other.

"SOON HOPE! YOU'RE GOING TO BE DEAD AND THIS KINGDOM WILL BE MINE UNTIL I DIE!!!"

"YOU'RE RIGHT IN ONE AREA!!!"

"WHAT'S THAT?!?!?"

"THIS KINGDOM IS YOURS UNTIL YOU DIE, HOWEVER YOUR DEATH IS GOING TO BE TONIGHT SETH JIMMY KINGSTON!!!!"

"USING FULL NAMES ARE WE? WELL THEN, IF YOU THINK YOU'RE GONNA WIN THIS FIGHT HOPE BREANNA KINGSTON THEN THINK AGAIN!!!"

Eventually the two run out of ammo from shooting each other and throw their guns, while Hope is able to avoid Seth's, he mistimes his dodge and it hits him in the head, causing him to go against the wall he was right infront of when behind the cover.

Seeing this opportunity to corner him, Hope rushes over and places her sword's tip on his neck, ready to stab it at a moment's notice.

"Heh, go ahead, you've won this battle apparently."

Something felt off, she didn't expect him to give up that easily, despite that however, she starts to interrogate him.

"Why'd you do it Seth? Why'd you really cause all this chaos and shit."

Instead of anything, he shrugs and speaks with his mouth closed.

"I don't know"

"ANSWER ME!"

The sword is pressed against his neck a big harder now, to the point where, although it's not alot, there is some blood starting to come out.

"Hehehehe."

"What's so funny?"

"Even if you kill me, i've won."

"How so?"

"Simple: Firstly, It would make you no better then me, killing someone who's also killed? Doesn't that take you down to my level? Wouldn't it be smarter to lock me up until I die, or something like that?"

"Secondly: If I die, this castle goes boom, with you and ANYONE in the vicinity of Edalbire being caught in the explosion."

"I would say to evacuate the city but by the looks of it, that's already happened."

"How do I know you're not bluffing? And i've never killed..."

"Hehe, you so sure about that? Why not say that to the many human guards of mine you killed before I replaced them with robots."

"Hell, why do you think I replaced them? They kept getting killed, not only by the rebellion but by you as well."

"Is that why you kidnapped our scientist?"

He starts clapping, however, instead of it being sincere, it's extremely sarcastic.

"Took ya long enough."

"WHAT HAPPENED TO HIM!!!"

"That's...actually, the one thing I can't answer."

"How do i know you're telling the truth."

"Because I would have mentioned it to you by now if I knew what happened."

"You have every right not to believe me, however I honestly have no idea what happened to him or how he escaped."

...Not in any position to argue, Hope looks at her brother, on the ground, ready to be executed.

"Oh well, talky time is over."

He does exactly what she did when she got up and as such, the two start clashing swords again.

A few minutes after that clash starts, Hope is able to get a stab into the arm which Seth is using his sword with, knowing that, that's his strong arm, she is able to get it in all the way through which causes him to scream out in pain.

The time: 18:00

With blood pooring out from Seth's arm, as well as it being completely unusable, he drops his sword and goes onto the ground, it seems as if Hope might actually win this fight.

Judgement Day 18:00-23:00

Hope was just standing there, her sword in her brother's arm and him screaming out in pain, once he had screamed enough, he takes her sword and points it at her brother's neck again, and to make sure he can't pull some bullshit, she proceeds to stand on his legs with some extreme pressure.

"You accept defeat? Seth Kingston?"

An evil smirk creeps onto his face, along with a quiet laugh, despite him still being in agonising pain.

Not a second after that laugh, he is able to brace himself for what's about to come, as Hope gets ready to swing her sword to slice off his head.

Much to her surprise, Seth is able to grab Hope's wrists with his free arm and as such, he pulls her off him, to her surprise, he's able to throw her to the ground.

"You forgot one thing Hope..."

He is saying this as he's applying a faux bandage from a part of his blazer that was ripped off earlier in the fight.

"...You forgot that i'm ambidextrous, sure, my right arm is now perma out of commission, but my left arm is still intact."

"You..."

The two start clashing swords again, this time with Seth's sword being on the opposite side of what it was before.

"Do you not have any bullshit hidden up your sleeve?"

"I can't help it if I actually came prepared to this fight and you just came with your weapons."

"You see, the thing is, yes offensive is important but so is defense, espically for a rookie like you."

While the extreme condescending tone from her own brother did piss her off, the thing that ultimatly pushed her over the edge....again

192

is him calling her a rookie, although he didn't know this, one of the things not to call Hope is a rookie.

She attempts to stab him in the stomach again, forgetting about the armour that's there and as such, Hope is sent flying back again.

Seth walks to her lying against the wall and sighs.

"You know, I could swear you were smarter then that...or did you let your leadership role get to your head?"

Before she can do anything, he steps on the hand that's holding the sword and rubs it with his foot, causing it to bleed and making her unable to grab anything with it.

To stay on the safe side and not wanting her to do what he did, he does the exact same thing with her other hand and as such, she is now unable to grab the sword at all.

Once her hands have been subdued, he walks a bit further into the room and starts speaking.

"You know Hope, from the day you left, all the way to day, I always thought that someday you'd step foot inside this castle."

"Hell, i'm honestly very surprised that your rebellion didn't figure out your true identity."

He goes back to her, bend down and grabs her chin.

"You could see it from space, the legendary Hockface was in reality, the rightful heir to Edalbire."

She responds, however she is in excruciating pain right now due to the hand thing Seth just did.

"So you admit it then...you admit you committed regicide and usurped the throne?"

"No? I didn't mention regicide, although now that you bring it up..."

He lifts her by the back of the head and takes her straight to the window, which he proceeds to smash.

Once it's smashed, he holds her by her collar and dangles her out the window, with heavy winds making it's way into the throne room, causing Seth's balance to wobble, however he is able to stay standing.

Meanwhile, Hope is just one grabless hand away from death.

"Yes, I did kill poor mummy and daddy, however, they deserved it."

Clearly now just playing with his kill, much like his other victims, Seth throws Hope back into the room and against a wall to the side that's near the window.

"You see, all they had to do, was hand the castle over to me and I would have taken Edalbire into it's golden age with them alive."

"They would be disgusted by what you've done."

"DISGUSTED? HA!"

"Nah, they'd be thrilled."

"Plus, you just had to wander in at the wrong time didn't you?"

"Well, i'll admit, I did hesitate a bit at first but once that sword went in dear old mummy's stomach....I FELT A RUSH LIKE I HAD NEVER FELT BEFORE!!!!"

"And without hesitation, not only did I kill poor old daddy but also most of their guards, annoyingly, one got away but, eh, thems the breaks."

"If only you didn't wander in when you did, I even had the perfect lie lined up for you and ready to go."

"I would have told you that they died peacefully in their sleep, however before that, I would have made sure the blood and all the bodies had been disposed of."

"You're not human...you're a fucking monster, no shread of humanity left in you whatsoever."

"You deserve to die."

"Maybe I do and maybe I don't, however, how do you intend to kill me? You've got no working hands so you can't use your weapons and if you try to push me, you'll only get sent back."

"You see, the way I see this is that i've won this fight and you've lost, you lost the moment you stepped foot in this room."

"Now, if only you had stayed back with your team, then maybe, just maybe you'd have stood a chance."

"But no, you had to be stubborn didn't you?"

"Oh well, not like i'm the one with a death wish."

"It's a shame too, you did have a bunch of strong soldiers, i'll give you that."

"Why..."

"Oh? Changing the topic are we? Well then, let's go."

"Why did you do it?"

"You know what, I may as well tell you...in fact, I can probably tell the whole world, I doubt the UN would be able to get me."

"Anyways, I did it cause of our parents."

"No...what's the real reason?"

"That is the real reason though..."

"You're lying..."

"..."

"I can tell you're lying, you had an ulterior motive for killing them."

"And why should I tell you?"

"Do you really think I'm in a position where I can tell anyone...?"

Out of nowhere, Hope starts coughing up blood, it seems that the fight has taken too much of a toll on her body.

"Damn, coughing up blood already? Can't have ya dying on me just yet, not after my story has been told..."

"So...you're going to say...?"

"Maybe? I don't know."

"However, I am intrigued to know more about your rebellion."

"Why...?"

"So I know how to stop the next one."

She chuckles very weakly, Hope has knocked on death's door and is now just waiting for someone to answer.

"As if i'd tell you..."

"Thought as much, oh well, I can just figure things out for next time, you know what, may as well drop this bombshell on ya now."

"What bombshell...?"

"So, have you heard of The Chaos Fighters by any chance?"

"You mean the violent world government agency...what about them...?"

"Well, here's a little fun fact for ya: Some of the rebellion's members were actually field agents for them and they very easily was able to infiltrate your ranks."

Hearing that causes Hope's eyes to widen in horror, of all the things to come out of her brother's mouth, that is something she never expected to hear.

"You're joking right...?"

"Nope."

He pulls up the official TCF headshots of...

Gothboy

Gasmask

Science Lab

Vetry

Bounty

and

Stopwatch

"These members of the rebellion were also agents for TCF."

"Why...?"

"Why what?"

"Why did they not say anything?"

"I don't know, multitude of reasons probably."

"Most likely, not even allowed to say anything."

"How do you know this anyway..."

"My informant."

" "
...

"Oh, don't worry, they're not anyone in the rebellion, i'd have killed them ages ago if that was the case."

"Then who...?"

"You may recognise their name..."

The next word to come out of his mouth makes Hope wish that the informant was a traitor to the rebellion, she'd much rather deal with that then...

"...Purge."

Just hearing that word alone is enough to send shivers down her spine.

"You're joking..."

"Nope, oh apparently, they had actually been a part of the agency for a few years now."

"And why should I believe you...?"

"You don't have to, you do know that you're gonna be dead very soon anyway, right?"

She coughs up blood again.

"It's a shame that our time is almost up Hope, I had really hoped that our fight could have gone on for a bit longer."

He looks at the time: 21:30.

"But hey, at least we have time for one more story, whatcha say?"

Instead of saying anything, she spits in his face, however instead of just saliva going onto his face, some of her blood is there as well.

He wipes the blood and saliva off his cheek.

"Well, I was going to let you choose the story but thanks to that, I'll choose it."

"Anyways, this fight got me wondering something: Why did I let you live instead of kill you?"

"For the answer...I'm honestly not quite sure myself."

"I...think I know...why..."

"Oh? Care to enlighten us?"

"Deep down...you wanted me to...dethrone you."

"Oooo, getting all psychological on us are we?"

Seth walks back to his sister to sit on the floor and look her in the eyes.

"I wonder, did you ever get a degree in psychology?"

"What's it to you?"

"Oh, nothing, just curious plus wanted to bond with my sister before she died."

"Bite me."

"No thanks, not a cannibal."

"Answer me some questions before you kill me..."

"Fine, may as well."

"What...happened to the guards you...executed?"

"So you knew about that? Anyway their bodies were disposed of and thrown into the ocean, I had no use for them so what else was I supposed to do with them?"

"Cremate them? Give them a burial?"

"Oh, those are boring though."

"..."

"What is the real reason you didn't you kill me years ago?"

"I don't know, I wish I did however, it would have saved my ass a whole lotta trouble."

"However..."

He gets up starts piercing his sword into her stomach, because of that, blood starts coming out from under her jacket.

"I can now do what I failed to do a few years ago."

Instead of responding, she's just coughing up blood again and trying really hard not to scream in pain.

"I know alot of people say this but how many can actually mean it...You're only delaying the inevitable."

Hope tries her hardest to get her sword from the ground, however to the mess that her hands are, she is unable to lift it up.

"Oh, naughty, naughty."

Even though he was going to do it anyway, he pushes his sword in even further, somehow, however, Hope is still not screaming in pain and instead she looks him in the eyes.

"You know, in an alternate universe, we could have been working together."

"W...w...why not....n...n...now..."

"Too late for that now, oh if only you didn't run away like the coward you are."

"Y...y...y...you're the c...c...coward."

She's struggling to get any words out at this point, Seth has point, from here, any moment she's alive, she's just delaying it, Death has already answered his door but now she refuses to go in.

Again, he pushes his sword into her, however this time, it's given enough power to come out of her back, at which point, he lifts up said sword and shows it off outside the window.

"You're a monster...you're g...g...g...going to pay..."

When she finishes saying that, Seth watches the life drain out of his sister's eyes until there's none in there, to make sure that she's dead, he puts the body on the ground and stabs her with the sword repeatidly.

Once the body has been stabbed many times to make sure that she's dead, he throws it out of the window and it lands on the ground with a really loud thump.

No-one in Edalbire can believe what they just witnessed, was it true? Did Seth really just win that fight? Is Hope Kingston and by extension the rebellion really dead?

There's no sounds coming from anyone on the streets or in any of the towns, cities and villages of Edalbire.

The only sounds are those of the wind and the news helicopters hovering in Edalbire.

"Take a good look Edalbire, now that the princess is dead, I am your ruler until the day I die!"

Like before, no sounds come from anyone.

"Wow, no standing ovation? Damn, tough crowd."

"Ooo, i'm probably never gonna get the opportunity to this again."

He runs back into the castle, gets some speakers and starts playing some rock music, that he sings along with his unique spin:

"I'm chilling on my throne in the hot sun, I fought the crown and I won, I fought the crown and I won."

"I turned the lives of innocent people to shit cause I wanted to, I fought the crown and I won, I thought the crown and I won"

"I left my family and it feels so good, I guess my race is on, I've had no girl and I don't care, I fought the crown and I won, I thought the law and I"

Instrumental

"Killin people with lies, I thought the law and I won, I thought the crown and I won"

"I lost no one and I gained my fun, I thought the crown and I won, I thought the crown and I won"

"I left my family and it feels so good, I guess my race is on, I've had no girl and I don't care, I fought the crown and I won, I fought the crown and I"

Instrumental

"I fought the crown and I won, I fought the crown and I won" x7

"I fought the crown and I"

No-one doesn't know what to say or do, all they can do right now is watch Seth gloat to hell and back while all the news helicopters head back to the countries they're broadcasting in.

Once the song ends, everything is just silent, no-one knows what to do...except.

"ROBOTS!"

"YES SIR!"

"BRING ME THE SURVIVING MEMBERS OF THE BLOOD RENEGADES!"

"RIGHT AWAY SIR!"

Not too long after, the robots each come back with a surviving member of the rebellion.

"Oh, this is gonna be fun."

Seth looks at the time now: 23:00

Epilogue: 23:00-00:00

The outskirts of Edalbire; what would usually be a beautiful landscape countryside with peace and quiet has that ruined, not only by the loudspeakers that can be heard from there but also by the helicopters leaving the country.

Standing on a hill are two beings: Science Lab, however, he doesn't have his lab jacket on and Proto.

"I hope they arrive soon, Proto..."

A worried beep comes from them as they're watching the live stream of Seth executing the remaining members of the rebellion in horror, despite being horrified by it, he can't bring himself to not watch it, well that is until he hears a familiar voice.

"Didn't ya know that the blue light from your phone is bad for your eyes at night?"

After hearing that voice Science Lab turns around with their phone's light in front of them and sees none other than Gothboy.

"GOTHBOY!"

He had never sounded so relieved and happy in his life, finding out that so far, one of his friends was still alive, during the hug he had started to cry.

While he was crying, Proto was beeping excitedly.

"H...h...how did you survive?"

"You're forgetting Henry... I've got no fears."

"I know but.."

He is able to regain his composure and wipe the tears from his face.

"Hey, remember those pills CF gave us?"

At first, Henry nods, and then his face turns to one of realisation.

"Yeah, they temporarily killed us, you didn't take yours?"

He pulls out a little capsule and inside it is the same small white pill that Gothboy took.

"I'm curious now: How did you get out?"

"Little word of advice for if you ever become a dictator? When you kidnap someone and chain them up with modern leg chains...make sure they don't know the person who programmed the software."

"Oh...wait, you could have broken out at any time?"

"Yep, I just wanted some insider information to relay over to the rebellion."

"I see."

"Anyways, where're the others?"

"Gasmask should be on her way now, not so sure about Vetry, Bounty and Stopwatch."

As if right on cue, those four show up together.

"Hey, how's it going?"

Bounty is the first to speak and once hearing that, Henry runs up to and hugs them all and despite not being much of a hugger, Gothboy does the same.

After they part from the hug, they all gather round in a circle and Gothboy is the first to speak.

"Hey guys, should we go back to first names?"

The other five agree to that.

"Alrighty...uhhh...remind me again?"

Gasmask: "Sophia"

Vetry: "Dylan"

Stopwatch: Alfie

Bounty: "Max"

Science Lab: "Henry"

Gothboy: "And finally me: Charlie"

"Noice, oh Gas-"

Charlie cuts herself off, she had intended to say Sophia's name but out of instinct, almost said her codename from the rebellion.

"Sophia, can I speak with you in private for a minute or two?"

"Okie."

The two go to some nearby trees.

"So, did you do what you wanted?"

Sophia nods.

"Mhmhm, they're safe in The Netherlands now, I know that for sure."

"That's amazing, I am so glad that your family was able to get out of Edalbire."

"Except..."

"Except what?"

"I don't know where Sapphire is."

"Oh..."

"Any news at CF HQ?"

"Nope, they don't know either."

"Well, I'm sure he's fine, plus he has an amazing sister, I'm sure he won't want to upset you."

Charlie places her hand on Sophia's shoulder and gives her a warm and wholesome smile.

"Heh...I always forget just how tall you are Charlie."

"Yeah, I get that."

"Then again, I am pretty small so, maybe it's also me?"

"Yeah, you're what, 5'2 aren't ya?"

"5'1"

"Damn, that is small"

The two make small talk in an attempt to cheer each other up, meanwhile the others are chatting about something more important.

With mainly Henry and Dylan speaking.

"So...how do you think they're gonna react when they find out the mission is a failure?"

"I don't know but I'm mostly scared of how Norman's gonna react."

"Oh boy, he's got his hands full with the eyepatch kid right? The last thing he needs is us coming back after a few years with a failed mission."

"Wouldn't that kid be like 18 or 19 now though?"

"True, still doesn't take away from the eye patch."

Charlie overhears the conversation they're having.

"Don't let Norman hear ya refer to Kenzey as 'Eyepatch kid.'"

Dylan is the first to respond after Charlie mentions that.

"Why not?"

"Uhhh...I made that mistake once....regretted it ever since."

"How so?"

"So, you know how in one game, there's a character who supposedly kills an innocent person and he's sent to this room with like 3 higher ranking people and one of them kicks a table?"

"Yeah?"

"Norman is worse than that."

"Oooookkkkkkkkaaaaayyyy then, not gonna ask any more follow-ups."

"Good."

"Anyways..."

Both Charlie and Sophia return to the group.

"...What now?"

"I don't know, probably best if we just bite the bullet and take whatever punishment we get."

"Oh boy...we were chosen for this mission cause all of us grew up in Edalbire and yet...we somehow failed."

The group start walking down the hill in silence, all deep in thought, heading away from Edalbire, until Alfie turns around.

"We'll come back and next time, we'll be ready for you Seth...just you wait..."

After saying that, the group starts walking back and Charlie pulls out her phone to ring a certain number.

"Hello, the Edalbire mission is over, requesting pick up from this phone's rough location."

Once she says that, she puts the phone down and the group just continue walking.

THE END?

Don't miss out!

Visit the website below and you can sign up to receive emails whenever Ashley Casey Tyrrell publishes a new book. There's no charge and no obligation.

https://books2read.com/r/B-A-TJSY-JZTJC

BOOKS 2 READ

Connecting independent readers to independent writers.